sugar & spice

SPICETOPIA

BOOK 1

PHOEBE ALEXANDER

Mountains Wanted Publishing

P.O. Box 1014

Georgetown, DE 19947

www.mountainswanted.com

Paperback ISBN: 978-1-949394-74-0

Cover design by the author

Editing and proofreading by Mountains Wanted Indie Author Services

❀ Created with Vellum

To all the single parents out there making the best lives possible for your kids.
Don't forget to take care of yourselves too!

one

"**A**nd that's why you're our first choice for going undercover in the park," my father announced, pinning his dark gaze on me.

"What?" I shook my head adamantly. "No, I'm going to Greece next month to study sculpture with Kristoph Kostopoulos."

"You can't go to Greece. You just went to Tahiti two months ago," my oldest brother, Carson, piped up from across the table. He turned toward our parents. "Cy hasn't done anything to support the business since he got out of college—which has been two years now!"

My middle brother, Clem, was quick to add his two cents: "It's about time you start pulling your weight around here, Cy. Last time I checked, we're all due to inherit an equal share of Sweet Enterprises, so it's time for you to step up."

My mother laid a soft hand on top of mine, forcing my eyes to snap to hers. "They're right, Cy. It's time for you to contribute. I know you're the youngest, and we've given you some time to 'find yourself,' or whatever you're calling it these days, but if you want to be part of the family business, you have to do your fair share of the work."

Heaving a sigh, I resigned myself to whatever this stupid plan was, but I wasn't done arguing my point just yet. "I don't think studying art means I'm not pulling my weight."

I couldn't help it if my family didn't understand all of my nerdy passions. Didn't they realize there's a lot more to life than some dumb children's theme park? I wanted more for myself. I had dreams, and they had nothing to do with running my parents' business.

My brows arched as I figured out how to "sell it" to them: "Maybe what I'm learning about sculpture can benefit the park in some way. Maybe I'll be able to design a new attraction someday?"

Carson rolled his eyes so hard at my sales pitch, just witnessing it gave me a headache.

My eyes darted between my parents, begging for their blessing. "Is there any chance I can wrap this assignment up quickly and still make it to Greece next month?"

"Tell you what," my father leaned toward me with his hands clasped together, index fingers steepled, "you infiltrate the employee clique and identify the ringleader threatening to organize a strike, and you'll not only get to Greece on time, but we'll give you a twenty-five-thousand-dollar bonus. Sound good?"

Oh, it did sound good. Very good indeed. A small smile curled my lips as the dollar signs sparkled in my mind. It wasn't about the money. I just really wanted to work with Kristoph Kostopoulos. Money wasn't everything, but it was a means to an end. And that end was me pursuing my passions.

Greece, here I come!

Confession: I'd never had a manual labor-type job, and I'd never worn a uniform. Being thrust into this role was giving me real *fish out of water* vibes, but I was trying to suck it up. All I had to do was identify the traitor, clue my parents in, and then I could take the sculpture course in Greece I'd already signed up for.

I may have had a reputation for being a partier, but I really did want to learn about sculpture. And Greek architecture. And just immerse myself in all that beautiful culture for a while.

But first…I had a transformation to make.

My parents had owned Sweetopia my entire life, and, every summer since I was sixteen, I'd worked a cushy summer job there, usually in "security." My brothers and I would sit high up in the control center at the top of Cotton Candy Castle and monitor all the cameras surveilling different areas of the park. Basically, we zoomed in on all the MILFs with spectacular cleavage. Nice work if you can get it.

I was particularly mortified to look in the mirror before heading into Sweetopia for my first day as Undercover Boss. This cheesy pink polo shirt emblazoned with the Sweetopia logo was pretty awful. But, even worse, I'd be forced to don a pink and white candy-striped apron to go over the entire ensemble. I looked like a Ken reject in the Barbie bargain bin at the local toy store.

No one could know my true identity, obviously.

No longer Cyrus Sweet, heir to the billion-dollar Sweetopia empire, I was now a regular seasonal employee in the bakery. The only people who knew about my undercover boss assignment were the ones in the boardroom when the decision was made: my mother, father, and my two older brothers.

I had to walk from the outer echelons of the employee parking lot into the park. Our family had a fleet of golf carts to carry us around the grounds, but, of course, I couldn't use one of those. I rolled my eyes at the absurdity of it all as I made the trek from my beat-up Dodge truck—my parents wouldn't let me drive my classic '69 Camaro—toward the huge fuchsia, purple, and teal arch that read SWEETOPIA in gigantic curlicue letters.

I stopped at the gate with my Sweetopia logo cap pulled down low on my face. My parents insisted I disguise my appearance, so I spent the last week growing some stubble. I also trimmed my shaggy dark hair, and my mom bought me a pair of black plastic-framed glasses with clear lenses. They didn't want anyone to have a single inkling that I was Cy Sweet. But who would ever guess my true identity when I currently looked like a hipster douchebag?

"Hi, I'm Marcus Young, reporting for duty," I chirped in a British accent, giving the Sweetopia employee at the gate a mock salute. *Where the fuck did that accent come from? I'm not British. Shit.*

Getting through this ordeal without my trademark sarcasm was going to be an Olympic-caliber feat. Maybe a British accent would help me be more proper?

The gatekeeper, a tall, lanky chap with huge gray-blue eyes, looked down at a clipboard. "Got ya," he said, barely glancing up at me. "Marcus Young. You're assigned to The Bard's Bakery in the—"

"I know where it is." I tried not to sound like an asshole, but I very much sounded like an asshole. A British one at that.

The skinny dude gave me a shrug, and I was on my merry way to Cotton Candy Castle, the spires of which gleamed silver in the morning sun. I stopped for just a moment to admire the way dawn splashed its golden splendor on the park. I was proud of this place, of my family's legacy. It was one of the top family attractions in the state, and my parents built it from the ground up. But that didn't mean I wanted to devote my whole life to this place when there was a beautiful world out there waiting for me to explore.

The Bard's Bakery was just inside the front entrance of the castle, where little girls and their families flocked to see The Red Velvet Queen. There was also a ride inside, one of those boat rides through a tunnel with piped-in music and animatronic characters. This particular ride showed how The Red Velvet Queen and her friend Donut Dragon defeated an evil sorceress to claim the throne of Sweetopia. It was a very empowering story. #Girlpower, et cetera.

I was headed straight to the bakery when I remembered that my oldest brother, who was in charge of casting for the park's costumed characters, hired a new Red Velvet Queen a few months ago. The one we'd had for years aged out of the role. My father decided we needed some fresh blood, and the veteran queen was asked to abdicate her throne.

Both Carson and Clem agreed the new Red Velvet Queen was hot—and they had notoriously different tastes. This naturally led to my own insatiable curiosity about her appearance. It wouldn't hurt to steal a glance to see if my brothers' story could be corroborated.

Tiptoeing down the hallway, I realized if any of the other employees caught me back here, I would be in "big trouble." I didn't want to make a bad impression on my first day—or blow my cover, but curiosity killed the cat and all that. I slowly pushed open the heavy doors that sealed off the queen's throne room and scanned the long, elegantly appointed chamber for...

My eyes landed right on the gold throne. There, regally

perched in the center of the plush crimson cushion was the most beautiful, elegant, royal creature I had ever seen in my life. Glossy black hair in big, sumptuous curls cascaded around her ivory shoulders, and lush, creamy décolletage spilled out the top of her red velvet corseted dress. She had the most exquisite full red lips, with a distinctive cupid's bow. Her nose, cheekbones, and graceful neck were sculpted by a master artist, and most entrancing of all were the glittering gemstones gazing at me from behind thick, dark lashes. Her perfectly groomed eyebrow shot up as soon as she saw me.

"Oh, sorry, wrong room!" I called out in that blasted British accent and went flying back through the doors as though I'd just seen a ghost. Okay, maybe not a ghost, but she definitely had to be a mythical creature of some sort.

I'd never been startled—or even slightly taken aback—by a woman's beauty before. There was a first time for everything, but I was simply in awe.

Maybe it was just the costume, but I'd never seen anyone or anything quite like her. Clem and Carson both claimed she was hot, but they failed to mention she was truly a goddess. Despite my lowly undercover stature as a seasonal bakery cashier, I would find a way to make her acquaintance —the sooner, the better.

No—screw waiting. I wasn't a waiting-around kind of guy. I'd go talk to her right the fuck now.

JOLIE

THE GUY WHO JUST CAME IN HERE HAS A BRITISH ACCENT. Where the hell are they getting these temp employees? Apparently hiring American doesn't mean anything to the Sweets.

My internal rant concluded, I erased any lingering thoughts about the rude interruption and tried to look regal as my colleagues fixed the red velvet curtains around my throne area and adjusted the lighting so it pierced straight into my retinas. I was usually half-blind by the end of my work day, and I couldn't even get vision insurance.

"You all ready, Jolie?" The throne room manager reached up to brush a stray hair out of my eye. "Our guests will be here any minute."

I nodded, affixing a royal smile to my face. I'd been warming up my wrists to perform my queenly wave approximately five zillion times throughout the course of the day. The hundreds of little girls (and a few little boys—don't want to leave them out), who made my throne room their first stop of the day in Sweetopia were the real die-hard fans. They'd read all the books. Seen all the cartoons. They probably owned a Red Velvet Queen doll or two. And a lot of the girls showed up wearing their own Red Velvet Queen dresses. It was an adorable sight, seeing them all lined up out the throne room door. They were always so excited to meet me, and I wanted to be everything they imagined I would be.

I only got the part of the Red Velvet Queen because I looked good in a corset, had a pretty face, and little kids weren't scared of me. *But trust me—I'm no queen.*

I was all set to greet my subjects when I noticed the British guy pushing through the red velvet curtains again. *What is this dude's problem?*

He gave me a sheepish smile, and I noticed he was cute in a quirky sort of way, with the beginnings of a beard and black plastic-rimmed glasses. He had that sort of hair that always looked a little tousled, long on top and like he'd been running his fingers through it all morning. And he looked younger than me, maybe mid-twenties? I sort of wanted to hear his accent again, but he appeared to be waiting for me to speak.

"Yes?" I hoped I could put him at ease. He was obviously new around here and probably a bit disoriented. This place could be overwhelming at first. I remembered my Sweetopia employee orientation all too well—or perhaps I should call it "my indoctrination."

He approached with his hand outstretched. "Good morning, I just wanted to introduce myself." He kept walking and talking, but when he reached me, he just stood there awkwardly with his hand sticking out, looking boyish and adorably nervous at the same time.

That accent sure does funny things to the area the V of this corset points toward.

I shook off that thought before taking his hand into mine. Otherwise, I didn't think he'd ever work up the courage to touch me. His eyes were glued to mine—he had absolutely no shyness when it came to eye contact.

His eyes were so deep and brown, I was afraid of getting lost in them, so I quickly averted my gaze to his lips. *Nope, that's a landmine too.*

His mouth was outlined in manly scruff and looked so damn kissable that I once again moved my focus, willing my eyes to land someplace that would allow me to keep my cool: the Sweetopia logo on his pink polo shirt.

Ah, yes, Sweetopia—nothing was more effective at dousing the flames of desire than the thought of the fucking Sweets and their fucking lame-ass evil corporate empire.

"Well, are you going to tell me your name?" I prompted him, getting into character as the kind, benevolent, but thoroughly kick-ass Red Velvet Queen.

He straightened up immediately, though he maintained a firm, masculine grip on my hand. "Yes, Your Majesty. I'm Marcus Young." His now-confident grin never faltered. "You may find me at The Bard's Bakery if you should ever require my services."

His services? And what might those be?

Stahp! I commanded my wayward imagination.

Then, he raised my hand to his mouth and pressed those beautiful plump lips against my skin, making my insides turn to goo.

"It's a pleasure to meet you, Marcus." I gave him my most regal nod of approval, while on the inside, I was busy stamping down all the flames incited by the combination of his looks, accent, and the feel of his lips on my skin.

If I could get my stupid body to calm the fuck down, I could focus on how nice it would be to have a polite, handsome gentleman over at the bakery. I couldn't visit during work hours, of course—what queen visited a bakery when there were servants to deliver anything she could possibly desire? But I already had a habit of stopping in before I got into costume and makeup. Even queens needed their coffee fix, after all.

"Oh, where are my manners? I'm The Red Velvet Queen," I announced in my royal voice, trying to stay in character. It was only seconds before the ropes dropped and my fangirls (and boys) came squealing into the throne room.

"I assure you, Your Highness, the pleasure is all mine..."

two

CY

It's a pleasure to meet you, Marcus.

Her words were still echoing in my head the entire time my new boss, Colleen, was trying to train me on how to operate the cash register. Who knew cash registers could be so fuckin' difficult to master?

This whole day had been a huge eye-opener to me, actually.

It was no secret I was born with a silver spoon in my mouth. Okay, maybe it was a big-ass silver spoon. But I also knew how hard my parents worked to build their empire. I didn't really remember them struggling, but I'd heard stories about them subsisting on ramen noodles when they first opened the park. They were able to secure a couple of loans that made all the difference, but my dad regularly pulled seventy-, eighty-hour work weeks when I was growing up. I hardly ever saw him. If I wanted to spend time with him, I had to go to Sweetopia.

Actually not a bad place for Take Your Kid to Work Day.

But the people in The Bard's Bakery, where I'd been placed for this whole undercover boss mission, they were really working their asses off too. This place was hopping from the time we opened the doors at nine this morning till we closed them at seven tonight.

I couldn't believe I just worked ten hours. I felt like I might collapse at any moment, whereas Colleen still looked fresh as a daisy, like she was just getting warmed up. She was used to this kind of work and putting in these long hours.

Whatever we paid these people, it was not enough. I'd have to speak to my father about that.

"So what did you think of your first day at Sweetopia, Marcus?" Colleen asked as she wiped down the stainless-steel counters in the prep area.

"Well, I thought—"

I forgot to use my accent. *Fuck.*

I repeated myself, this time with a heavier sprinkling of British spice. "It was bloody busy in here, but I think I caught on right quick, if I do say so myself!"

Colleen's lips quirked up, but it seemed like she was suppressing an eye roll. "Well, hope you'll come back tomorrow," was all she said.

I shrugged. "I don't have much of a choice, to tell you the truth."

And that was definitely the truth. Twenty-five G's on the line was a pretty big incentive. Not to mention staying in my parents' good graces.

I lifted the candy-striped apron over my head and set it on the counter. Was The Red Velvet Queen still perched on her throne? I hadn't been able to get the image of her with her long black hair, the feel of her delicate hand in mine. or the softness of her skin against my lips out of my head all day.

"So now what?" I asked Colleen, who was still standing

there looking at me like she'd never seen a dude take off an apron before.

She laughed and shook her head. "Now you can leave, Marcus. I'll see you tomorrow."

That was weird. I gave her a fake salute and hightailed it out of the bakery, trying not to slip on the sparkling clean tiles I'd just mopped. I had never used a mop before. Colleen, in her infinite patience, had to show me how. No wonder she was looking at me like I was a freak of nature. *Who doesn't know how to use a mop, right?*

In seconds, I made it out into the main corridor of Cotton Candy Castle. To my right was the entrance for the boat ride I mentioned earlier. Straight ahead was the queue for the throne room where the beautiful queen I'd met earlier might still be lingering. Guess where I headed?

I had to see if she was still there.

I parted the plush red velvet curtains and walked down the crimson and gold carpet that led to the shiny gold jewel-encrusted throne. I'd never noticed the exquisite craftsmanship of this piece in all my visits to the throne room, and I certainly didn't notice this morning when I was here. At the time, I couldn't take my eyes off the gorgeous woman perched upon it. I was so overwhelmed by her beauty, it actually took me a few moments to get my swagger on so I could talk to her and not sound like a complete idiot. It was literally the first time that has ever happened to me in the history of all my flirtations—and trust me, there have been a great many.

She liked me though; I was sure of it. I didn't know why I chose to cop a British accent for this undercover role, but the Man Upstairs must have known a beautiful lady was waiting to be seduced by it. And by Man Upstairs, I didn't mean my father, whose office was on the top floor of the castle. I meant a Higher Power.

I scanned the throne room looking for her, but it appeared to be empty. It was just as well because I knew there were cameras mounted in the corners of the room, and if we did end up conversing—or other activities—I really didn't want my brothers, who were now in charge of park security and HR respectively, to know about it.

My curiosity still running rampant, I decided to peek behind the curtains, so to speak. I'd never been back there, but I knew The Red Velvet Queen had a dressing room. A staff lounge and staging area for other employees were also on the other side. Those rooms connected to the underground tunnels the staff used to get from building to building, avoiding the crowds.

I just needed to find the entrance, and sure enough, once I lifted the heavy fabric, the metal door was just waiting to be opened. When I twisted the handle and found it unlocked, a bolt of excitement spiked from the top of my head all the way down to my fingers and toes.

It didn't take me long to get my bearings. The dressing room door was standing wide open. That probably meant the queen had already left for the day, but when I got to the door, I noticed her ample backside sticking up, set off by the narrow, tight laces of her corset as she bent over. I couldn't be bothered to ascertain what she was doing because tearing my eyes away from her gloriously curvy ass was an impossible feat.

So, allow me to clarify something right here and now: skinny girls with waify, boyish figures were not my jam. I'd always had a sincere appreciation for curves—the curvier the better. I was a student and lover of fine art, and, in my estimation, nothing was finer art than full, mouthwatering breasts and a juicy, fleshy ass. I subscribed to the Sir Mix-a-Lot theory of the feminine physique: "Baby got back."

"Oh!" She whipped around, the shock on her face flipping a primal switch deep inside me.

There was no denying my rampant desire to bend her over that counter, hike up those many layers of her elegant gown and have my way with her. And if I'd been able to introduce myself as Cyrus Sweet, one-third heir to the Sweet Enterprises fortune, I'd be able to pull off that maneuver with flying colors.

But I'd already introduced myself as Marcus Young, summer temp bakery cashier. This was a problem. *A big problem.*

"Marcus?" she gasped, her body vibrating with surprise. She dropped the purse she'd just retrieved as if she couldn't quite get her fingers and lips to work in tandem.

"I'll get it." I moved toward her, swiftly grabbing the bright yellow canvas pocketbook from the dark green carpet before lifting it into her still-trembling hand.

"I didn't think anyone else was here," she admitted. "Normally I'm not so paranoid."

"It's fine…" At least I remembered the British accent this time. By the end of my mission, it would be second nature to me. Maybe I'd take it to Greece when I went to study sculpture. Were Greek women as enamored with British accents as American women were? Probably not. After all, they had Greek men to fancy. I hoped I could compete, but I could always fall back on the whole being rich thing to woo any Grecian goddesses I encountered.

"Are you lost or something?" She scanned my face, blatantly searching for my motives.

Why was I creeping around her dressing room, I'm sure she wanted to know. But when she caught the smoldering look in my eyes, her mouth curled into a smile.

I was close enough now I could see the details of her features: the pronounced Cupid's bow of her lips, her delicate nose and cheekbones, the curve of her arched brows, and her thick-lashed eyes that were a silvery gray, nearly lavender color, a stark contrast with her raven locks.

She was exquisite, radiant, even after working all day. I wondered if she had her own makeup team who came in to freshen up her face during breaks. What did she look like under her Red Velvet Queen façade; were those black curls falling gently onto her bare shoulders natural?

I didn't care one way or the other, though. I wanted her, and I was pretty sure she could tell. Furthermore, I was pretty sure the feeling was mutual.

A worldly, wanton look shone from her silver eyes as I continued to assess her, my gaze wandering up and down her figure as though I were studying art at the Louvre, which I'd done during a semester abroad. She seemed to enjoy the attention; it was probably a welcome change from having millions of snot-nosed kids stare at her all day.

"Marcus?" she repeated—because I hadn't answered her question, had I?

"I *am* lost…actually," I admitted with more confidence than I should've had while wearing this god-awful pink polo shirt, "…lost in your eyes, that is. They are such an unusual color."

She let out the very tiniest scoff, as if she couldn't believe I had the audacity to toss out such a ridiculous attempt at flirting. But then her features softened as she soaked up my cheesy line like a sponge. "Are you heading home for the evening?"

I wanted to kiss away every word that appeared on her lips. How could I leverage this without blowing my cover?

"How long have you been The Red Velvet Queen?" I asked instead of responding to her inquiry.

"About six months." She cocked her head. "Why?"

"It seems like a role you were born to play." I reached out, gesturing for her hand, which she surrendered to me with a skeptical look, but a surrender nonetheless. I spun her around in place, watching her voluminous velvet skirt rustle around her legs. Oh, how I wished to know what those legs looked like…if the skin was as soft and porcelain-white as her shoulders and the elegant curve of her neck.

"You certainly have a way with words, don't you?" She shook her head, trying to hide her smile. "Are you really British?"

"Do you think I'd come in here and fake a British accent?" I retorted.

I mean, would I? Of course I would.

She giggled. "I don't suppose so." Her gaze swept up my body again, and the smile remained, proving she liked what she saw. "I do need to go, though…"

"Do you want to grab a drink?" As soon as I asked, I realized what a horrible idea it was, considering I was driving that god-awful beat-up truck. I would rather have a sharp stick poked in my eye than drive her around in that thing. Maybe I could negotiate with my parents to drive a nicer car tomorrow. Something a little more understated but still classy. *The Acura or the Infiniti? Clem has an older-model Lexus in his garage he's not using…*

"I can't." Her smile faded, reflecting genuine disappointment. "I need to get home. I'm really sorry. Raincheck?"

"Would you think I was crazy if I asked for a goodbye kiss?" I blurted out.

I had never been turned down for a kiss, and though I didn't have the cash or family fame to back up my request like usual, I did have the accent and the beginnings of a beard. From what I understood, most women were defenseless to these things.

"You are *quite* forward, Marcus." She took one step closer to me, her silver-violet gaze bouncing between my eyes and my lips. It was a good sign. "What is it you do here at the park?"

She'd probably seen so many faces today, she couldn't even remember the conversation we had this morning. That was lucky for me—I wouldn't have to admit I was a cashier at the bakery down the hall.

"Never mind that… Work is done for the day. So let's not think about it again till tomorrow." I reached out to stroke a finger down her cheek, but before I made contact, she visibly bristled.

Oh, shit. I might be going too far. This pink polo shirt screams pathetic loser, doesn't it?

"I'm sorry, may I?" I corrected myself. *Manners never hurt anyone, right?*

JOLIE

Calling security did very briefly cross my mind when Marcus went to touch my face.

Who the hell is this guy? I'd never seen him before this morning, and I had a feeling he was one of the new summer temps. I heard they never stick around long. When he evaded my question, I was even more convinced he was a temp.

He was not only persistent, but strikingly gorgeous with his sunkissed-tan skin, dark tousled hair, matching scruff outlining a strong jaw, and, of course, glasses. Glasses on a guy were always a total swoon-worthy thing for me. I always imagined it meant they liked to read. Probably a bad assumption on my part, but nerds had always been my type.

He stood there staring at me, waiting for permission to kiss me. The look on his face was a cross between boyish incorrigibility and devious scoundrel—a combination that was virtually impossible for me to resist.

And I wasn't used to someone else making the first move. In my other line of work, I called all the shots. I made all the demands.

Otherwise, it felt like a lifetime since I experienced anything close to intimacy. Anything close to this attraction pulling me toward him like a magnet—and I was doing a shitty job at resisting the pull.

He didn't repeat himself, but his eyes stayed steadily on mine, peeling away layer after layer of my possible defenses. It was clear the moment I softened, the precise second I surrendered, because a smile curled on his plump, luscious lips as he reached for my cheek again. A gentle touch tilted my chin up to receive his feathery brush against my mouth.

It was so much lighter and more delicate than I ever imagined. I let out a surprised gasp as he swept me up in his arms and deepened the kiss to something that, if I had ever experienced anything so passionate, it had been countless lifetimes ago.

His kiss was ravenous and needy, his arms tightening around my waist as his firm chest pressed into the boning in my corset, squeezing the air out of my lungs. Then his other hand threaded itself through my long, curly hair, pulling my head back to expose my neck. Seconds later, his mouth marched down my chin to my throat with nips and nibbles delivered along the way. My knees buckled under the weight of my full skirts and his relentless kisses.

Fearing I might collapse, I gasped again, the air filling my lungs with just enough oxygen to demand I take control of the situation. I jerked back, leaving him in mid-kiss, his eyes slowly fluttering open as if to ask *what just happened?*

"I'm sorry." His voice was a deep growl, as if he wasn't

actually sorry at all. "I just lost all control there for a moment."

The worst part was…so did I.

I wasn't the type to lose control. Both of my jobs—well, actually, all *three* of my jobs—were based on my ability to maintain control. Strict, unwavering control over my thoughts, my body, and my goals.

"Marcus," I simultaneously straightened my back and tugged down my corset, which had inched upward during our entanglement, "I really must be going." I stepped out of my velvet skirt and petticoat, leaving the corset on, then threw a long, shapeless dress over my head. "Can you find your way out?"

He nodded as my head poked out the neckline of the dress, but his lips were toying with a smile, as if he didn't believe I was actually going to leave.

"Maybe I'll see you around." I confirmed I was truly leaving by collecting my belongings and heading out the dressing room door. Security would lock up after me.

"But you didn't tell me your real name," he called after me.

I thought about tossing my name over my shoulder as I made my way through the labyrinth backstage area of the castle, but I thought better of it. A seasonal worker was a distraction I didn't need.

I had things to do. People to see. Battles to fight.

"Yes, Mistress."

The whip cracked over my sub's crinkled, sallow skin with a sharp pop that almost snapped me back to reality. I had spent the entire drive over here trying to get myself in the right frame of mind for my session with Mr. Barry, but I had failed miserably.

I couldn't get that kiss I shared with Marcus out of my head.

The one that started with the light-as-a-feather brush against my lips like an artist just barely dabbing paint onto the canvas.

So meticulous. So exacting.

And then the gradual, sweeping crescendo, the way every nerve was engaged, Marcus the Maestro conducting my body like an orchestra that swelled under his touch. Those tingles were still coursing through me, and it had been nearly an hour now since I fled down the dark hallway of the castle, hoping to god I didn't run into any of my coworkers.

I was afraid they would see the desire written all over my face.

"Mistress?"

Mr. Barry's pale gray eyes looked up at me as I walked around him. He was waiting for my next command. He was waiting to get his money's worth.

I pushed the thoughts of Marcus deep down into my soul and mustered up that raw, unyielding grit I'd practically trademarked. *I can get through this. I will get through this.*

LATER THAT NIGHT WHEN I PULLED INTO THE LAST OPEN parking space in the apartment complex, I rushed up the stairs to my front door. The porch light had burned out. Again. *I swear, it's always something.*

I unlocked the door and tiptoed in. It was nearly ten o'clock, and my mother was sprawled out on the sofa. She stirred when she heard me approach, even though I was trying hard to be quiet.

"Go to bed, Mom," I whispered.

"How was everything?" Her voice sounded groggy.

It was so hard for her to sleep, I hated waking her up. I'd tried to be quiet, but these thigh-high lace-up boots with four-inch spike heels were not exactly conducive to sneaking around.

I couldn't wait to get out of my second costume for the day and just breathe free, no restrictive laces or boning digging into my ribs. I just wanted to be naked. But I'd have to coax Mom into her own room first.

"I'm fine, Mom." I gestured for her to follow me. "How was River tonight?"

She smiled, putting on her own brave face. *Where do you think I learned it from?* "He was coughing earlier, but he quieted down eventually."

I sighed. I hoped he didn't have another fit tonight. We'd had to use his nebulizer in the middle of the night twice last week.

I really needed to sleep tonight. We all did. Tomorrow was another long, grueling day.

After getting Mom settled, I slipped out of my boots, relishing the feel of the cool linoleum under my stocking-clad feet. This time when I tiptoed, I barely made a sound.

River didn't stir when I traipsed across his carpeted floor and bent to check on his breathing. There was a slight rattle in his lungs that never fully went away, but otherwise, he seemed fine. His older brother, Reed, stirred, pulling the blanket back around him as he flipped over to face the wall.

"Love you," I whispered into the dark room. I hoped their little ears picked up my voice and carried it into their dreams.

three

CY

Last night, my father called me into his office to remind me of my mission in the park: to determine which employee was organizing meetings and possibly planning a strike or some other type of retaliation. I had a feeling he wanted to get rid of whoever this trouble-maker was before any further damage could be done to employee morale or our family's reputation.

"I'm working on it, Dad," I sneered at him. "I've only been there one day. Cut me some slack."

His mouth set into a firm, thin line. "I just know you have a tendency to get off-track, Cy," he admonished me. "Like how you switched your major three times in college, and how one minute you're in Tahiti studying Polynesian art, and the next minute you want to jet off to Greece."

"I know, Dad." I rested my hand on his shoulder. "But having that money you promised will really help me make the most of my trip to Greece. It's a powerful motivator.

Today was just getting the lay of the land. I'll start actual reconnaissance and putting feelers out tomorrow."

"Okay, Son," he fixed his dark eyes on me, "don't let me down."

That conversation was still ringing in my ears when I pushed open the back door to the castle and weaved through the labyrinth of tunnels and hallways until I made it to The Bard's Bakery.

"See? I made it back!" I waved to Colleen, my boss, before I reached beneath the counter to pull out the apron I'd tucked under there the night before.

"If you're looking for your apron, it's hung in the back room where it belongs. Hooks to the right of the freezer," she told me flatly.

"Oh, okay, sorry. Guess I forgot." At least I hadn't forgotten my British accent today!

She seemed to accept my sheepish smirk with a tilt of her head and just the faintest hint of a smile. I came out of the back room tying the apron around my waist. It was time to ooze charm and start gathering some intel.

I scrubbed down my hands in the stainless-steel sink. "So how long have you been working here?" My accent was especially thick today. Thanks to my British roommate in college and a couple of trips across the pond, it was pretty damn natural-sounding too.

"I'm coming up on my eighth anniversary," she answered, "so you could say I'm a Sweetopia vet."

I observed as she began to roll out some dough, admiring the way she had all the cookie cutters lined up on the counter ready to be used. There was a crown, a castle, a throne and a dragon. I only knew those were the cookies we sold because I saw the finished products yesterday. It was pretty unbelievable that this big mound of dough could be transformed into something so detailed and intricate-looking.

"Have you always worked in the bakery?" I continued, trying to get her to loosen up. She was friendly enough, but I could feel tension radiating off her.

"I worked in the ticket office my first year." She wiped her flour-covered hands on her apron. "What about you? Is this your first job?"

"Oh, well…" I stammered. I didn't want to talk about me. "Sort of. I just graduated from college." It was a lie, but it would help explain my lack of job experience.

"Uh huh," was her reply.

Like I said, she was nice enough, but she gave off serious disapproval vibes. It was almost like hanging out with my parents, though I was pretty sure she wasn't old enough to be my mom. She was probably…late thirties? Early forties? I wasn't good at guessing stuff like that. She had shoulder-length reddish-brown hair and kind brown eyes.

I glanced down at her hands as she began to press the cookie cutters into the dough and move the sliced cookies to a large metal tray. Her hands were chafed and raw, like they'd been washed too many times, and she wore a modest diamond engagement ring and matching silver band on her left hand. *So, she's married.* I was starting to feel like a regular Sherlock Holmes.

"Are you happy working here?" I proceeded with my investigation. I couldn't exactly take notes, so I would need to commit all of this to memory. Maybe I needed to get a recording app for my phone?

She let out a sigh as she grabbed the rolling pin off the flour-dusted counter. "It was better when I first started."

"Oh yeah? Why is that?" I pushed a little harder.

"Can you quit gawking at me and put that tray in the

oven?" She nudged her head to the commercial ovens stacked in the corner at the end of the counter.

"Oh, yeah, of course." I grabbed the tray and moseyed down to the oven. I assumed the one with the orange light on was the one it needed to go in. I couldn't recall ever putting anything in an oven, nor taking anything out, for that matter.

Here goes nothing! I gritted my teeth and pulled down the door, sliding the tray neatly inside. I didn't know why I was surprised to be hit with a blast of heat—ovens are supposed to be hot.

My face was still on fire when I noticed The Red Velvet Queen herself had entered the bakery. I whirled to find her staring at...pretty sure it was my ass. Since I had to bend over to use the oven.

Naturally, that reminded me of seeing her bend over the day before. And what a sight it was.

Then, not only was my face on fire, but a warm, tingly sensation crept down into my more southerly regions as well. When I met her gaze—a cool, lavender frost—my dick sprang to life. What was it about this woman? She seemed to have a command over my manhood like no other woman I'd ever encountered.

"Hi," I choked out, remembering my accent right after the word left my mouth. "Cheerio," I corrected myself. *That's British, right?*

A gorgeous crystalline laugh spilled out of her mouth as she threw her head back. Her raven curls rustled around her shoulders as she continued to giggle. Then she shot a look at Colleen, who had begun to join in her amusement.

I'd nearly forgotten the conversation I was having with Colleen—or that Colleen was even in the room—until she brought the queen up to speed on our conversation. "Marcus was just asking me what I thought of working for Sweet Enterprises."

I detected more than a little sarcasm in her voice. *Maybe Colleen is the infidel?* I hoped not though. I really liked her—so far.

"How should I answer that for the newbie?" Colleen continued, her head tilted to the side and her lips pursed.

"You know what they say," the queen brushed a wide swath of her hair off her shoulders, letting it fall against her smooth, bare back, "honesty is the best policy."

Oh, yes, now I was getting somewhere. If Colleen wasn't the insubordinate one, perhaps she or the queen knew who was leading the revolt. It was apparent they had a beef or two with the company.

Also, I desperately needed to know this siren's name. I couldn't keep calling her "Queen." Maybe I could call her "Red" for Red Velvet? *But she has black hair.* Okay, maybe "Velvet," then.

My mind kept spinning, completely losing myself in her beauty. "Hot Stuff" also seemed to suit. Or perhaps "The Cock Whisperer," since mine seemed to be completely under her control.

I was so engrossed in coming up with potential names for this goddess in front of me that I nearly missed Colleen's answer to my question:

"Sweet Enterprises masquerades as a family company, but, in fact, they're one of the worst companies in America for families. Their health insurance sucks, the vacation packages and sick leave suck, and most of their employees make minimum wage."

"Velvet" shot my boss a look. I couldn't quite interpret it, but it appeared to be a mix of agreement and trepidation.

I gulped. "That doesn't sound good."

"Be glad you're a temp," Colleen said, "and that you just got your college degree. I'm sure you'll find a great job with your—" She looked me up and down. "What kind of degree did you say you have?"

"Art history," I choked out.

Now the two of them exchanged knowing looks, and their thoughts on my chosen area of scholarship became abundantly clear.

"Never mind," Colleen said with a laugh. "You may be here for a while, kid." She finished pouring some coffee into a large cup, popped a lid on it, and slid it across the counter to the waiting queen.

Velvet's frosty amethyst eyes were still dancing with amusement when she picked the coffee up from the counter and took a sip. She flashed them over to me, and apparently that jolt of caffeine was all it took to remove any traces of mirth from her exquisite face. I couldn't help but notice her intense stare seemed to be spiked with something else...

I was struggling to put my finger on it, but when the corners of her lips pulled up seductively, and her teeth sank into her bottom lip, I realized what it was:

Desire.

JOLIE

That guy in the bakery was a trip. I had coffee this morning before I left the apartment, but I fully admit I stopped by the bakery for another round just to see if Marcus was there. I didn't know what it was about him—the glasses or the accent—but he was simply adorable in a much-too-young-for-me way.

I hadn't been able to get the memory of his lips on mine out of my head since our kiss last night. He was so forward, so assertive. Definitely not what I expected from someone still in his twenties, not to mention someone meeting me for the first time while I was decked out in my Red Velvet Queen ensemble. Most men I met were a little standoffish in general, and the ones I met in costume—including the most dashing single dads—were even more intimidated.

But not Marcus. After he got past the initial awe of my royal splendor, he went right after what he wanted. I had to admire that—and wonder if there was more where that came from.

The way his eyes lit up when he saw me proved thoughts of our kiss had been floating around in his head as well. But now I needed to push those thoughts to the back of my mind so I could go about my day and be the queen my little subjects needed. I had to admit I was struggling with the idea of sitting on that throne all day, and seeing him again didn't help. But at least the extra caffeine might allow me to recapture my focus.

As I climbed onto my throne, arranging my voluminous red velvet skirt around my legs, I wondered how I was going to muster up the enthusiasm I needed to get through another long-ass day of smiling, hugging children, and acting all regal and shit.

I'm doing it for Reed and River, I reminded myself. *My precious sons. My lifeblood. My everything.*

With my renewed sense of purpose, the morning shift went faster than I expected. My assistant roped off the entrance to the throne room and announced to everyone in line that we would resume the meet and greets in an hour.

A month into my tenure at Sweetopia, I had to beg and plead with my bosses for an hour lunch break. They only wanted to give me thirty minutes, with no other breaks throughout the day. I was pretty sure that was illegal, but the Sweets didn't care much about labor laws. I was always working overtime, staying when the line to meet me was way out the door. I hated disappointing all those kids. Did I get paid time and a half for that kind of devotion? *Hell to the no.*

Trying not to let the rage spark inside me, as it tended to do when I thought of the Sweets, I lifted my sore ass off the throne and made my way behind the curtains to my dressing room. Imagine my surprise when I saw none other than Marcus from the bakery leaning against the counter, evidently waiting for me with a salacious grin on his face.

"What are you doing here?" My voice came out much higher-pitched than I was hoping for. *What happened to the low, breathy regal voice I use in the throne room?*

"You ran off last night without telling me your name." He straightened to his full height, which looked to be a very solid six-foot-two.

I'd never seen a Sweetopia employee look sexy in their stupid candy-pink polo shirt, but Marcus obliterated that record. His biceps filled out the short sleeves, the cuffs tight around his firm, sculpted, bronze-colored muscles. And now, with his apron off, I could see the shirt was stretched a little tight across his pecs. I had a feeling rock-hard abs lurked beneath that fabric.

Marcus was such a stark contrast to my clients, most of whom were pasty-white older men with small dicks and receding hairlines. They had money, though. So at least there was that. Their money and predilection for discreet discipline and humiliation were essential in filling the gaps my salary here at Sweetopia left, especially when it came to caring for my special needs son.

"Sorry about that." I dipped down to retrieve my lunch from the small refrigerator under the counter—another amenity I had to beg my bosses for. His eyes burned into my backside before I rose to meet his gaze again. "Do you mind? I'm supposed to eat lunch now."

"I'm hungry too," he fired back, but it was obvious he wasn't talking about food.

This guy was so completely ridiculous, I had to bite back my laughter. I was used to my subs. They were eager to please and so demure. I wasn't used to interacting with a man who was so…assertive. Aggressive.

I hated to admit it.

I mean, really, really hated to admit it.

But I like it.

As much as I tried to deny it—hell, I worked as a dominatrix, for fuck's sake—I liked an alpha male. And a smart, charming, glasses-wearing alpha male? With a fucking British accent, no less? Well, I was done for.

Of course, that "type" was exactly what got me into so much trouble in the past. That was why I had two sons and no man to show for my efforts. Both of their fathers skipped town before they were even born.

Assholes.

My tubes were tied now, though. There weren't going to be any accidental pregnancies. Besides, I was a lot smarter now than I was when I was twenty-one and twenty-five respectively. I was now thirty-two and knew better than to let my heart out of its cage again. That ship had sailed.

Marcus must have taken my quizzical look as an invitation because he stepped closer to me. His dark eyes were aflame as he stroked a long finger down my cheek. "I haven't been able to stop thinking about you since last night."

I stifled a giggle. "Is that so?"

But…being thirty-two and completely opposed to any type of relationship didn't mean I couldn't have fun. *Right?*

"Yes, Your Highness, it is so," he growled in that fucking panty-wetting British accent. Though he insisted it was, I doubted it was real. Not that I cared. It was still sexy as fuck. "But I still don't know your name."

It wasn't like he couldn't find out my name from his boss or any other park employee. I rolled my eyes before settling them on his, which were dark and flickering with desire. "It's Jolie."

"Jolie," he repeated. "What a beautiful name."

"Well, yeah, it means 'pretty' in French," I snapped back.

"I know." His upper lip quirked before he sank his teeth into his lower lip. "I know French."

"You do?"

"*Oui, madame.*" He gave me his most charming smile and swept down into a bow.

He was too. Fucking. Much. I wanted those lips on me.

I hadn't had a summer fling in years. Not since college. I hadn't even had real sex in a year. *A year!* There were probably dust bunnies in my vaj.

And, no, for the record, I didn't have intercourse with my BDSM clients. My work as a mistress was purely about discipline: spanking, whipping, restraints, orgasm denial. Fun stuff like that.

Despite all that, I knew I shouldn't go any further with Marcus. I should have just sent him away right then, should have waved him off dismissively. It was beyond stupid to get involved with someone at work—especially with everything I had on the line here at Sweetopia.

But he was a summer temp. If we could just make it through the next three months without anyone finding out, he'd be out of my hair. And I could have a little fun in the meantime, a little distraction from my grueling life as a single mom with two jobs and two sons, one of whom had special needs.

"Come here," I beckoned him with my index finger curled and wiggling.

He pointed to himself with an innocent grin, like, *who me? Yes, you. Get your ass over here*, I said with my eyes.

In two steps, he closed the gap between us, and a heart-beat later, his arms were wrapping around me. There was a strength there, a sense of control that set my nerves on fire. Even through all the layers of my costume, I felt my lady bits soaking my panties as his lips crashed into mine. His grip on the back of my corset was so tight, and my breasts heaved so frantically, I thought the entire bodice might burst open at any moment.

"Just a second." I broke away, desperate to make sure my dressing room door was locked.

It was.

My mind swirled with all sorts of devious thoughts as he swept me up in his embrace again, his lips feverishly working against mine, then attacking my neck and down to my cleavage. My makeup artist was going to have her work cut out for her restoring my face to its former regal glory at the end of my lunch hour.

He lifted me up onto the counter, not even slightly balking at my weight or the absurdity of so many flouncing layers of velvet and lace. I expected him to ask me how to gain access, but he was silent. He simply lifted and parted. The cool air from the vent above my head hit my pussy with a whoosh, a lightning bolt cascading through the raging inferno it had become.

"What are you doing?" I breathed out, my chest still heaving as I struggled to fill my restricted lungs with air. *Damn, this corset is so fucking tight!*

"Having lunch," he murmured matter-of-factly as he hooked his fingers on the sides of my black satin panties and slid them down my legs.

There was no time for me to say anything else before his mouth claimed my dripping pussy lips, the scruff of his beard grazing against the delicate tissue and sending a series of brilliant tingles up and down my spine. My clit began to ache for his tongue as he spent what felt like hours lavishing the rest of my womanhood with attention. As I threaded my fingers through his dark hair, my hips bucked against his face, and his chuckle vibrated through me.

"Patience, my dear Queen," his deep voice rumbled. "I want to savor every last drop."

But I couldn't think straight. My hips were involuntarily grinding into him, my grip tightening in his hair. *Fuck...where did this man learn to eat pussy?* It was like he'd taken a class. Like he could teach a class.

Sometimes I made my subs pleasure me, but it was rarely pleasurable. It was all for them. They wanted to be scolded, punished for not doing it adequately. They were sloppy and ineffectual. Marcus was a goddamn master.

"Fuck..." I was so close to the edge. When was my last orgasm? It was by my own hand, no doubt—and it was so fuzzy, I couldn't remember any of the details.

As if I weren't already teetering, he inserted one, then another finger into my tight channel and began to fuck me relentlessly with them. He lifted his head up just far enough to say, "Come for me, Jolie. Come all over my face."

That did it.

A burst of ecstasy shot through me like a rocket, shattering the steadily rising walls of need his tongue had built within me. I felt a gush as each spasm clenched around his fingers, which had stilled to bear witness to my climax. I was off somewhere beyond the moon, having a lovely visit before slowly floating back down to earth.

The orgasm relinquished its command of my body, and my senses began to function again. I noticed for the first time that my fingers were nearly numb from gripping the edge of the countertop, and my lacy petticoats were itchy around my hips. Marcus panted as he finished slurping up the mess I'd made.

"That was—" I started to eke out.

"No." He lifted himself to standing, then he leaned over to press a finger to my lips. "Just go eat your lunch. You need to keep up your energy for your queenly duties." He winked as he stepped back and offered me a hand to help me to my feet.

Is this guy even for real?

"Don't you want…?"

He shook his head. "Enjoy the rest of your afternoon."

And in a flash, he was gone.

four

CY

I dutifully passed on the intel I'd gathered to my parents, who only implored me to push harder. The only thing I wanted to push hard was my throbbing dick into Jolie's wet pussy, but she ended up calling out sick the rest of the week.

I couldn't get that woman out of my mind, and her not being there made my week that much longer and more grueling. Every time I thought about her, I pitched a tent in my goddamn pants like a freaking teenager. I had never—EVER—been affected by a woman this way.

I had also never gone down on a woman and not expected anything in return. I needed to see if she was as beautiful moaning and quivering in pleasure as she was just looking at me with those mesmerizing lavender-gray eyes.

The truth was that she was even *more* beautiful.

After spending most of my weekend sleeping, because a full forty-hour workweek kicked my pathetic ass, I parked my piece-of-shit truck in the employee parking lot at Sweetopia and began the long trek to the gates. Naturally, the sky opened up just as I made it far enough from the truck to make going back for an umbrella wildly impractical. Typical Florida weather.

As my shirt soaked through, I thought about stripping it off and venturing down to the throne room. Maybe Jolie would enjoy watching me strut around in all my shirtless glory. Maybe I could have my way with her before the clock struck nine and the park was invaded by zillions of rambunctious, sugar-fueled kids.

Maybe we at least had enough time for her to reciprocate the oral I gave her last week? A little tit for tat, so to speak.

I would be happy if she was just back at work, to be honest. I would be happy just getting to see her again. All those hours I slept over the weekend? They were filled with dreams of a voluptuous goddess with raven locks and silvery violet eyes.

I headed for the back of the park where the fancifully pink Cotton Candy Castle jutted into the cloud-layered sky. A momentary worry about lightning striking one of the spires flashed through my mind, but it faded when I noticed the throne room door was open today.

Her absence last week—that was another thing my parents were livid about. The Red Velvet Queen had called off work for three days straight.

"We need to hire an understudy," my mother insisted. "She's the most popular costumed character. Do you know how disappointed every single little girl in the park has been the past three days? Some parents wanted refunds just because she wasn't here!"

My father just grumbled something about how expensive it would be to keep an understudy on staff. Then my mother followed up with a rant about how maybe they should fire the current queen and find someone more reliable.

The way they were talking about her made me so angry, but I couldn't say anything. And I couldn't say anything to Jolie either, or I'd blow my cover.

It appeared she had returned, however, because the throne room doors that had been shut the past three days were now open. A huge sign expressing Sweetopia's sincerest apologies that the attraction was temporarily closed had rested on an ornate golden easel in front of the locked doors. It was gone now.

I would go say hi as soon as I clocked in. I was running late. *Damn rain.* I hoped my boss wouldn't be too mad.

I sneaked in the back door, weaving through the kitchen before making my way to the counter area of the bakery. Colleen was facing away from me, speaking with someone on the other side of the counter.

My eyes immediately snapped to Jolie, looking absolutely divine in her tightly corseted red velvet gown as she chatted animatedly with my boss. The only thing missing from her usual ensemble was her crown. I was surprised they let her come in here in costume.

I had the sudden desire to take her while she wore nothing but her jewel-encrusted tiara. That would be fucking sexy as hell.

I stopped short when I overheard their conversation.

"—that's another thing we'll talk about at our next meeting," Jolie said.

"Are you sure you're going to be able to make it? Everything is okay at home?" I detected worry in my boss's voice.

Jolie let out a sigh. "As far as I know. There's too much at stake at this point..."

Colleen nodded. "I know it's hard." She laid her hand on top of Jolie's, which was perched on the countertop. "Are you sure there's nothing I can do to help?"

A lump formed in my throat. *What is going on with her?*

From the way her brows were bunched up and her lips were pursed, it seemed like something pretty serious.

"No, but thank you, Colleen. I hope everything comes together like we've all planned. I know we're not alone. And there's so much support for this, not just here but...more broadly." Jolie's cheeks rose as a hopeful smile spread across them.

"Amen to that," my boss agreed, patting Jolie's hand again. "Well, we're going to keep the faith and keep fighting."

"Always." Jolie's features brightened as her clenched fist rose in an expression of solidarity. Then her gaze jerked up to find me standing behind Colleen, tying my apron around my waist. "Well, if it isn't Marcus!" She shot a warning glare at Colleen, but I couldn't read my boss's reaction as I stepped out into the main service area of the bakery.

"Good morning, ladies." I dusted off my British accent, which had gotten rather rusty over the weekend. I'd nearly forgotten my glasses when I left my house today. Thank god I remembered at the last minute.

"Did you have a nice weekend?" Jolie questioned, but she didn't really wait for an answer. Instead, her eyes flitted toward the clock before flashing back to Colleen. "Shit, I have to go. I'll catch you guys later." With that, she gathered up her full skirts and scurried across the bakery, exiting out the side door into the castle.

I aimed my thumb in the direction she went. "Is everything okay with her? I noticed she was gone a few days last week."

Colleen sighed, her worried look only deepening. "I hope so..." was all she said, her voice trailing off somewhere her words didn't want to follow.

I shrugged. "So what is this big meeting about?" I tried to slide that question in there as nonchalantly as possible. *So stealthy and undercover bosslike of me, huh?*

Unfortunately, my boss waved her hand to dismiss my question. "Oh, nothing. Don't worry about it."

But I *was* worried about it. I had a feeling Colleen was hiding a great deal of valuable intel from me. I told her I'd be right back and headed to the bathroom, but my plan was to stop any Sweetopia employee I saw and ask if they knew anything about some "meeting." *Strategery and all that.*

First guy I encountered was a janitor of some sort. He was running one of those manual vacuum thingies (*no idea what they're called; my knowledge of household appliances is sorely lacking*) down the carpet runner that led to the throne room.

"Hey," I said as casually as I could.

He looked up at me with a blank expression. He was young, maybe eighteen, and he wore braces.

When it became apparent he wasn't going to return my salutation, I asked, "Do you know anything about the next meeting?"

"Meeting?" He scratched a bit of sparse scruff on his chin that had nothing on the sexy beard I was currently cultivating. "Sorry, bruh. Don't know what you're talking about."

"Okay, thanks." I flashed him a smile, but his only response was to raise an eyebrow at me before shifting his gaze back to the carpet runner.

I continued down the hall until I came to the gift shop. This place was about to be overrun with children, so I felt like I was on the clock. I mean, I was *literally* on the clock, of course. But also now figuratively.

Hopefully, I could swoop in and out and not have to deal with a massive stampede to buy a plush Donut Dragon, the friendly creature that lived in Cotton Candy Castle with The Red Velvet Queen. The dragon was the loveable sidekick that helped the queen defeat the evil sorceress and save Sweetopia from peril.

I spotted the store manager, but panic surged through me

when I considered asking her about the meeting. She looked familiar, and I was pretty sure I met her a few summers ago when I was working "security" or maybe at one of our company picnics.

Would she recognize me? It was a risk I'd have to take. My trip to Greece and a large sum of money were on the line.

Ambling up to the counter, I channeled my nerdy, unassuming temp worker persona. Slouching a bit should keep me from swaggering in like I was Cy Sweet and practically owned the place. I coaxed the British accent into overdrive as I introduced myself. "Hello, I'm Marcus Young. I'm over in The Bard's Bakery. Just trying to get around to meet everyone else in the building. How are you?"

The way she smiled at me, it was obvious she was checking me out. She was several years older than me, but she still had good taste, right?

"I'm Ellie Martin." She extended her hand for me to shake, the interest in her honey-brown eyes unmistakable.

"It's nice to meet you, Ellie." So much for the "unassuming" vibe I was going for. The words slid out of my mouth with so much charm and sex appeal that I practically made myself swoon. I needed to tamp down the Cy Sweet before she recognized me.

"We don't get too many Brits in these parts," she said with a wink. *An actual wink—swear to god!* "What brings you across the pond?"

"Oh, you know, university…" I offered a flirty smile, hoping I could use her attraction to my advantage to leverage some information about this meeting Jolie and Colleen were discussing. *I might be able to figure out the company's Benedict Arnold today. Greece, here I come!*

"Florida Gulf Coast?" she mentioned the closest school to the park.

"Oh, sure," I agreed, still smiling and hoping she didn't ask any specifics. I went out of state and didn't know much about any of the local colleges.

"Nice, what are you studying?"

Shit. I should have known she would make this all about me. "Hey, I have to get back to the bakery before Colleen sends out a search party. I was just wondering something, though?"

"What's that?" Her eyes sparkled as though she was expecting me to ask her for a date. *Yeah, right!*

I cleared my throat and leaned in closer. "Do you know anything about a…meeting…coming up?"

Her nose, which was a little too large for her face, wrinkled up, showing her extreme disappointment. She swallowed it down and forced a smile to lift the corners of her lips. "Yeah, why?"

Oh, fantastic, now we are getting somewhere!

"Where is it? Who's organizing it?" I pressed, trying not to seem too anxious for the answers—even though I was practically desperate for them.

She giggled. "It's by invite only, sorry. Can't reveal my sources." She gave me a wink that was too flirty to be anything but an invitation to probe a little deeper.

"Oh, well, how do I get on the invite list?" I smiled as if I understood what she was getting at and still wanted to play along.

"I might be able to give you some info about it. Come back and see me tomorrow. We've gotta open the doors now."

"Great, thank you." I blew her a kiss on my way out. *Won't hurt, right?*

I wasn't above a little man-whore action to get to the bottom of this employee uprising thing—and to get my twenty-five Gs, of course.

JOLIE

"HE'S GOING TO HAVE TO GO BACK TO THE DOCTOR," my mom sighed as she met me at the door. I hadn't even taken off my crown yet—that was how fast I rushed home.

"He's still running a fever?" I checked.

When she nodded, I brushed past her to get to River, who was sprawled out on the sofa watching his favorite cartoon. I pressed my lips to his forehead and immediately felt the heat soak into me.

"Can you take tomorrow off?" Mom asked in the vocal equivalent of a tiptoe.

I whipped around. "No, I'm already in enough trouble. Fucking Sweet Enterprises." As soon as the words were out of my mouth, I closed my eyes as I bit my lip in frustration. "Sorry, guys. Don't use that word, please. It's only for adults."

"Why the fuck not?" my son Reed quipped. *Of course.* At ten, he was always pushing my buttons. And Lord knew he didn't get enough attention with his brother's issues always shoving him aside.

"Look," I shot him a warning glare, "I'm doing the best I can. I have an appointment tonight, and I can't cancel it, so I have to go get changed."

"But you were gone last night," my mother reminded me.

I huffed, trying to blow out my growing exasperation. Maybe if I stripped out of this corset, I would be able to breathe again. But I was only going to be exchanging this corset for another. My clients wouldn't know what to think if I didn't show up in my black latex corset and boots, my expected Domme attire. At least I didn't have to wear that godforsaken wig.

I marched off to my room to execute my costume change. My mother always had to help me with the corset I used for my sessions with my subs. She would be in shortly. I had two or three seconds to take a deep, unrestricted breath before being laced up again.

"Jolie," Mom started up again as she closed my bedroom door behind her, "you're going to have to find a job with better benefits and leave. River needs his mom around. So does Reed, for that matter."

She reached for my hand and squeezed it in hers. I knew she was trying not to cry, but the tears glistening there anyway, threatening to fall. At least the boys couldn't see or hear us. If there was one thing I tried my damnedest to do, it was keeping them from knowing how tough things really were for our little family.

"You think I don't know that?" I argued with her. Heaving a sigh, I scrubbed my hands down my face. "But I haven't been able to find anything that pays as well and offers any benefits at all. Or anything that might actually help my acting career. It's not like I haven't tried."

She shifted her gaze to the floor and sucked in a steadying breath before looking up at me again. My mom had given me my unique gray eyes, but hers were lighter than mine. They seemed to have faded at the same time her hair lightened into a silvery blonde. She was washing out before my very eyes, trading her youth for more time with River.

A tear streaked down her cheek. "River's not going to be here forever."

Her tears were reserved for me in private. And mine were reserved for her. In private. We couldn't let those two young men in the other room know the depths of our despair. Our helplessness. Our constant pleadings with God for more time, more strength, more money.

"Mom..." I couldn't bear for her to start up the waterworks right now. Not when I had to change clothes and leave for my other job. "I'm doing the best I can. We have some things in the works at Sweetopia. We're having a big meeting soon, and we're about to go to the media with our demands. I think things are on the cusp of changing. Everything's coming together..."

"You said that three months ago," my mother fired back. Her lips pursed as her eyes bounced back and forth between mine. "And last year when you were still at Barney's."

"What is it you want me to do, Mom?" I begged of her. "Please, tell me. Because I can't help that I'm a single mom who gets zero support from the two loser sperm donors I fucked. And I can't help that my kid has cystic fibrosis. There's literally not a *damn* thing I can do about any of that."

"Jolie..." My mom took my hand into hers again. "I know you're doing the best you can. You're so beautiful and talented. I just feel like you should be able to find an employer who really respects you and will compensate you accordingly—and not make you feel guilty when you need to take off a few days to care for your sick kid."

"Yeah, it takes a lot of talent to sit on a throne and pose for pictures all day." I rolled my eyes. "Please."

"You're selling yourself short. You're playing a role you were born to play. You make an amazing queen, Jolie. No one would guess in a million years you're a single mom scrounging up her last few dimes to fill up the gas tank and supporting a household of four on two jobs. When you put on that crown, you become The Red Velvet Queen. Through and through. The Sweets would never be able to replace you. They'd never be able to find someone who embodies the role like you do."

"Thanks, Mom…but I don't need a pep talk. I need to get changed for my other job."

But my words didn't deter my mother, who was at least three times more headstrong than I was. "And even though it still weirds me out, I bet you are amazing in that—other role—you perform too."

I rolled my eyes. She couldn't say the word "dominatrix."

"You need a real acting job," she insisted. "A TV show, a movie. Hell, even commercials to start with. You're not getting any younger, Jolie. You need to look for an agent again and put yourself out there."

"And how do you propose I do that when I'm already working sixty hours a week? Besides, if I play my cards right, I can take this Red Velvet gig right onto the big screen. You know they're talking about a live action movie. What else can I do but wait it out?"

My mother shook her head. She didn't have an answer for that one. Sure, I'd always dreamed of being an actress, but I'd never made it any further than the stage at my high school and one or two community productions. None of those roles paid, anyway. What I did now were the only two roles I could take on that actually did pay a salary. It was the best I could do under the circumstances.

And on that note, I needed to get going before my sub left me for a mistress he could rely on to show up on time.

THAT NIGHT AS I LAY IN BED, I WAS OVERCOME WITH SADNESS. There was just no way in hell I could make everyone happy: my bosses, my sons, my mother. Someone always got the short end of the stick. The stick being me, of course.

And I was always the biggest loser. I always gave of myself until I had nothing left to give.

I had no friends outside of coworkers. I had nothing for myself. I couldn't even remember the last time I had fun.

And then, I did remember.

The memory slammed into me so hard, I nearly fell off the bed. Marcus the week before in my dressing room. He'd appeared out of nowhere, and all he wanted to do was see me writhing in ecstasy. He was so damn talented with his hands, his tongue. Those dark eyes. That tousled hair. The scruff on his sculpted jaw.

The entire encounter only lasted what, fifteen or twenty minutes? But he made it all about me. And the look on his face when he made me come? Pure exhilaration. He was so happy he gave me pleasure.

Seeing him today at the bakery, the confusion and concern on his face when he walked in on me discussing my situation with Colleen, it was so sweet. He seemed like such a giving, sensitive guy. I needed a man like that in my life. Even if it was just to have fun with. He was obviously younger than me, but he was definitely into me. There was no denying that.

What if I asked him on a proper date? What if I let him see the real me? The me minus the crown and plus a hell of a lot of baggage?

Would he still want me then?

five

JOLIE

I needed something to get me through the day, and coffee was just not going to cut it. My mother was taking River back to the doctor, and I couldn't go because Sweet Enterprises was headed by the devil himself: Corden Sweet. Oh, and his evil fucking wife, though I couldn't remember her name. I heard their three sons also worked in the park, so apparently nepotism was A-OK, but allowing the mother of a sick child to care for said child was not.

Fuck them. Fuck all of them.

I did briefly consider dumping some Bailey's into my coffee, but it wasn't like I had any. I didn't have any alcohol in the house and no time to stop for some. I didn't even think I could find a liquor store open this early. So I went to work, and I knew damn well what I needed to do.

It was like he knew.

He was waiting for me in the hallway right outside my dressing room. Marcus Young, propping himself up, all tall and lean, against the concrete block wall that was painted cotton candy pink like half the other surfaces in Sweetopia. It was a color that made my stomach churn at this point.

"Well, good morning, beautiful." His lips curled up as he drank in the sight of me. "Where'd you run off to last night? I wanted to talk to you."

"Did you?" I tried to keep my own mouth from mirroring his smile, but it was a pointless endeavor. He made me smile against my will, especially the way he enunciated "beautiful" in his sexy-as-fuck accent.

I fumbled with the key in the lock. Men didn't make me nervous. I told them what to do—*I* made *them* nervous. But that didn't hold true for Marcus. Even though he was younger than me. Even though he was just a summer temp in the bakery, he had a commanding presence, one that seemed completely incongruous with that blasted pink polo he was wearing.

Well, there was one way to solve that problem. I'd rip it off him the first chance I got. I couldn't deny I'd already been thinking about doing that for days.

"Need help?" I could feel his eyes on me, boring into me as I finally got the key to engage and managed to swing the door open.

"Not with the key." I whirled around to meet his gaze.

His eyes were doing that smoldering thing again. You'd never imagine it was only eight in the morning. He looked ready and raring to go. *Giddy up!*

"Have you been thinking about our little encounter the other day?" He reached up to brush some of my hair back away from my face. His accent was so thick and raspy, it was proper and gravelly all at the same time. How did he do that? It was fucking magic.

"As a matter of fact, I have been thinking about returning the favor," I admitted, locking my eyes with his.

"Do you often get fucked in your dressing room?" I could practically see the wicked thoughts swirling in his eyes as the question left his lips.

I let out the tiniest laugh. "No. I've never been fucked in my dressing room. Not unless the lunch you had last week counts…"

He pulled me into his arms, capturing me before whipping me around and pushing me up against the wall in one fluid motion. "There's a first time for everything…" His lips lingered by my collarbone as he spoke, each word punctuated with a little hot breath that made my skin even more inflamed.

The heat spread from my cheeks, down to my breasts, and surged to my core. Marcus was pressing against me so insistently, I should have been able to feel his erection—but, alas, it was impossible with this full skirt on. But it was a package I couldn't wait to unwrap.

But I didn't want him to see me naked. Not yet.

My corset covered a multitude of issues: stretch marks, sagging skin, a c-section scar. I was a mother. What most of society saw as "flaws" were an accepted part of my body— and I wasn't ashamed of them—

Well, I wasn't *exactly* ashamed of them. Okay, *mostly* not ashamed…

A man like Marcus Young, someone just out of college, was surely used to women his own age. Svelte, lithe, nubile women. Twenty-somethings with unblemished skin and firm, smooth breasts and hips.

I wanted to stay The Red Velvet Queen. I wanted to be his royal fantasy. I wished he'd hike up my skirts and have his way with me like he did last week.

But that pink polo shirt of his was coming off. *That is non-negotiable.*

I tugged at the hem, and he shrugged out of it like his

limbs were made of rubber. Raking my eyes up and down his gorgeous torso left me breathless. Two firm mounds of pecs were topped by pert nipples, with an exquisitely rippled set of washboard abs below. His arm muscles were well-defined, strong. And possibly the most delicious thing of all was the trail of dark hair that led from his mouthwatering vee into the khaki uniform pants that hung low on his hips.

"See anything you like?" He gave me a cocky smirk, though he knew damn well I was already eye-fucking him.

"I think you have some more work to do." I pointed at his belt as I bit my lower lip.

"What about you?" His eyebrow quirked. "I'll show you mine if you show me yours…" His growl tapered off as he nipped at my neck again, another burst of desire shooting through me.

"I can't take the corset off. I'll never get it back on in time to start work. It's a process," I explained. "Do you have a condom?"

His lips curled up as he nodded. Then he shook his head and gently slid my breasts out the top of the corset so they rested, full and heavy, against the velvet fabric. He appeared pleased with this compromise. "So, that's it, you're ready for me? No foreplay?"

"Undo your belt. Put the condom on. Insert Tab A into Slot B," I commanded him. I gritted my teeth as he reached up to pinch my nipple between his fingers. "Oww!"

I wasn't used to pain. Well, I wasn't used to *experiencing* pain, only *inflicting* it. The sharp sting seared through me but only electrified the need building in my core that much more.

"Don't get mouthy with me," he unbuckled his belt, "and you might want to reconsider taking this without any foreplay."

When he dropped his pants, I tried not to gawk at the massive tool he pulled out of his boxer briefs. He had to be at least eight or nine inches long, but that wasn't even the most noteworthy thing about his cock. It looked almost as big around as my arm, and it was striped with thick, throbbing veins.

I gulped down the shock I was desperately trying to conceal. It now made perfect sense, how this mere summer temp could have such a massive ego. It was an ego fed by a ginormous dick. He was definitely packing more than enough heat to back up his arrogance.

"Reconsidering?" He smirked at me as he reached down to stroke his erection slowly from base to tip. He squeezed at the end and revealed a glistening pearl of pre-cum.

"Just fuck me," I reiterated, knowing I was wet enough. I could feel it. The air duct over my head was blowing cool air right onto my pussy, and the sensation combined with the heat emanating from inside me was dizzying. Maddening. I needed him inside me *pronto allegro*.

I watched him roll the condom down his cock before he pressed the tip to my aching lips. He gyrated his hips, smoothly working that gigantic tool inside me, and the look on his face alone nearly made me come. His jaw was set in a firm, determined clench, and his eyes fluttered closed in ecstasy as he sank into my heat inch by inch. It looked like an agonizing mix of heaven and hell until I relaxed enough to take him in his entirety.

Then, as though the restraint was killing him, he reached for my chin, directing my eyes to his. "You okay?"

"Move!" I screamed, unable to handle any further delay. "Fuck me, Marcus."

"Be careful what you wish for," he fired back as he began to rail into me, hitting my cervix so hard, I nearly fainted from the sudden stabbing pain. It was only a moment before it began to feel good, just like how he'd tweaked my nipples before.

Here I thought I only enjoyed inflicting pain, but it seemed like I enjoyed receiving it too. How had I never discovered that before?

"Goddamn, you're so fucking wet," he growled into my ear as he continued his assault on my pussy. I wrapped my arms around him, digging my scarlet fingernails into the firm flesh of his ass to drive him faster, deeper.

I hadn't been fucked for a long time, and I'd forgotten how fucking glorious it was. How it demolished all other thoughts, all other pain. It was transcendental. I was floating on another plane of existence, spouting off some real philosophical shit, but my body was doing its thing, and I was about to explode.

Every fiber of my being was singing like a diva giving a sold-out concert at Carnegie Hall. This is what I had been missing in my life. This was what my body was built to do.

"Come on my cock," Marcus commanded as he gripped my hair and pulled my head back to gain access to my throat. He nibbled his way over to claim my lips, ravishing me in a fit of passion so intense, my pussy exploded around him.

"You're fucking milking me," he groaned as he stilled, feeling my walls spasm around him. "Can't. Hold. Back."

As the purple starburst behind my eyes brightened to reveal the soft lights of my dressing room, I caught sight of his body as it jerked out the last few spurts of his release. His face wore an expression of pure bliss, his head thrown back and sweat glistening on his brow.

"Fuck, Jolie," he slowly regained consciousness, "I was not expecting that this morning…"

My eyebrows arched. "Oh yeah? What were you expecting?"

He chuckled as he pulled his cock from my body and

stripped off the condom. "I think I expected you to at least put up a fight."

His comment made me a little miffed. I was no shrinking violet, and I refused to play coy. If that was what he wanted, he needed to go back to the co-eds he left behind in college.

"No…no, no, no," he insisted. He grasped my chin, tilting my face toward his and pinning his dark gaze on me. "I didn't mean that as anything but a compliment. I love that you know what you want and go after it."

I blinked twice. "You do?"

He nodded. "Oh, yeah, it's hot as hell. I'd always heard ol—"

I just knew he wasn't about to call me "older" after blowing a load in my pussy. I shot a warning glare at him.

"Uh, what I mean is that—"

"Mmmhmmm." He was adorable when he was flustered. The cockiness from earlier had vanished into thin air. "How old are you, Marcus?"

"I'm twenty-six," he revealed.

"Oh…"

And here I thought I was getting a twenty-two-year-old… twenty-three tops. He was just now graduating? What did he do, change his major five times?

"What? Did you think I was older?" Now there was a hint of embarrassment on his face.

"No…younger." I crossed my arms over my chest. Glancing up at the clock, I could see I was going to be late if I didn't wrap this up. I couldn't believe we fucked so damn fast.

"So, you aren't going to tell me how old *you* are?" He scanned my face with his boyish grin as if his charm alone could make me reveal the answer.

I squinted at him. "Are you really asking Her Majesty to

admit her age?" My index finger popped up, wagging at him. "Surely not."

A sheepish smile lifted his cheeks before his gaze fell to his watch. "Oh, shit…it's almost nine. I gotta run."

"Toodle-doo!" I called after him.

Thirty-two—that was the answer. Not that it was any of his business. He didn't need to know anything about me other than my name and how to make me scream his.

CY

"I'm getting close," I filled my parents in. "If the damn bakery wasn't so busy, and my boss didn't watch me like a hawk, I could get around to other parts of the park and gather some more intel."

"So, there's a meeting soon? That's what you know so far?" My father scratched at his chin as his eyes bounced between my mother and me.

"That's all you've found out?" My mother didn't bother to hide her disappointment.

I nodded. "No one wants to give up the organizer's name, but if I can just figure out when and where the meeting is, I'll show up and see for myself." I snapped my fingers as an idea came to me. "Can't you call my boss out of the bakery for a couple hours? Assign her an administrative duty of some sort? There are two other employees there most of the day. I could slip out and head over to Jellybean Junction or Marshmallow Manor to see if anyone there has information."

"The reason we stationed you in Cotton Candy Castle is because we're pretty sure the organizer is there," my dad explained. "It may even be Colleen. You're sure she hasn't said anything else about the company? Good or bad. We want to hear it all."

"It's clear she's not happy, but she doesn't sound like she's organizing a revolt either." I definitely didn't want to pin anything on her. I'd only worked there a couple of weeks, but I sorta liked her. She was a real down-to-earth lady, and I respected that. She was also good at her job, and, thanks to her, that bakery ran like a well-oiled machine. My parents were lucky to have someone like her on their payroll.

"You need to get closer to her," my mother interjected. "Grill her a little more. She's the ticket. She's been there long enough that she knows everything going on at the park. Even if she's not the organizer, she knows who is. I guarantee it."

"I met with our PR guy today, and he told me again he's seen some rumblings of 'disenchantment'—that's what he called it—on social media. There's apparently some secret forum on Facebook or something. You should try to infiltrate that."

"If your PR guy knows that much, then why can't he find out more?" I fired back.

"He can't seem to get definitive answers as to the ringleader…or ringleaders, plural. But he somehow discovered someone from Sweetopia is talking to a reporter at the local television station. We just don't know who it is."

My mother covered her face with her palms as if she couldn't bear to hear the rest of my father's statement. It was too alarming, too upsetting for her delicate sensibilities. I had to restrain my eye roll.

"But I don't understand why they would go to the media. What is so bad about working here?" It was only my second week, and it *was* hard work, but there was a sense of camaraderie I already felt a part of, and everyone seemed to enjoy making the kids so happy. Hell, I didn't even like kids, yet I still got a goofy grin on my face every time I saw a kid's eyes bug open at the array of sweets we offered at the bakery.

My dad shook his head. The vein in his neck was pulsating, a sure sign he was at the end of his rope. "I have given these damn employees my entire life! Don't they know how hard your mother and I work to make sure they have good jobs, fair pay, and a nice environment to work in? Ungrateful bastards!"

"Now, Corden," my mother admonished him. "Settle down. Do you want me to call William up here for another scotch?"

"Yes, please." My dad rubbed his temples as he paced back and forth between his desk and the huge floor-to-ceiling bookcases in his opulent office. This was his home office, not the equally luxurious one at the top of Cotton Candy Castle. It had almost as many amenities, but not quite as nice of a view.

My mother pressed down on the intercom and summoned William from the other room. He appeared almost immediately. "Please bring Mr. Sweet another scotch. And I'll take an amaretto sour, please." That was my mother's signature drink.

William nodded curtly and disappeared to fulfill his duties as my parents' butler or manservant or whatever the hell he was called. All I knew was that William and Maureen, our housekeeper and cook, had been working for my parents in some capacity for as long as I could remember.

Even in all that time, my parents still referred to each other as Mr. and Mrs. Sweet in front of them. *Weird, right?*

"When were you planning to leave for Greece?" My father paced back to his desk and collapsed in the plush leather executive chair. My mother took over the pacing, crossing back and forth in front of the window overlooking their nicely landscaped back yard.

"In two weeks," I responded without even thinking. But just after I said it, I got a weird pang of sadness that I would be leaving my undercover gig.

Even if Marcus was a lame-ass in an apron serving pastries all day, it was still kind of fun to be part of something. I enjoyed Colleen and the other folks I worked with. And sneaking into Jolie's dressing room every chance I got would certainly be missed. I hadn't stopped thinking about her once since that first time I saw her sitting on the throne.

"Well, you better hurry up and figure out what's happening at this meeting then, Son," my dad's voice slashed through my thoughts. "Time is running out. If you can't seal the deal and identify the ringleader before your trip, you won't be going. Not if you want to stay on the Sweetopia payroll and keep your inheritance."

I didn't appreciate my father's threat, but a flash of Jolie's heaving breasts as I feasted upon her pussy lit up my memory. Suddenly the thought of going to Greece seemed infinitely less exciting. I would have to get my fill of her before I left.

JOLIE

Holy shit.

Just climbing down from my throne at the end of the day, soreness pulsed through me. I had not only used muscles I apparently forgot I had, but my pussy was throbbing with a deep ache where Marcus's cock had thoroughly plowed my lady garden.

"You okay?" My assistant offered me her hand when I wobbled a bit on my dismount.

You would think the Sweets would hire an assistant who could take care of me, defend me, if a guest got a little out of control. You know, someone with a security background, who could protect me if I ever needed it. I greeted thousands of guests every day. It wasn't so far-fetched that one might go a little too far, even if they were well-meaning. And what if someone didn't have good intentions at all?

But, no, my assistant was this tiny young woman. She was about twenty-two years old and was about half my size. She couldn't protect me from a fly, let alone a raging drunk guest. That was one of my fears working here. I even mentioned it to my boss one time, and she laughed it off.

The motherfucking Sweets. They didn't care about employee safety. They didn't care about anything but their own greed.

"Your Majesty?" My assistant captured my attention away from the rant building in my mind.

"Yes, sorry. I'm fine." I smiled as my feet pressed into the thick, plush carpeting of the throne room. She had been instructed to never call me by my real name. Even backstage in the dressing room, she called me "Your Majesty."

She followed me through the velvet curtains to my dressing room. I heaved a sigh as she opened the door. I didn't expect to see Colleen sitting in the chair in the corner.

My hands flew to my mouth to stifle a gasp when I noticed her. "Fuck, you startled me!"

"Sorry, let myself in. I needed to talk to you about a few details that have come up." She stood and walked over to the counter where I sat for makeup. "Were you in the bakery earlier today?"

"No, why?" I met her dark gaze as she examined a Sweet-opia coffee cup in the corner of the counter.

"I just didn't remember you coming in, that's all." She

smiled and continued to go over her concerns with me about our upcoming meeting.

I couldn't take my eyes off the coffee cup she'd pointed out. It wasn't mine. And my assistant didn't drink coffee. She only drank energy drinks. She kept a stash of them in the small refrigerator here in my dressing room.

Did Marcus leave a coffee cup when he was here this morning? I didn't remember him having one with him.

"Jolie, are you listening to me?" Colleen's voice rose from the soft whisper she'd been using to discuss the meeting with me.

"Sorry…I'm in la-la land today." Once Marcus entered my mind, I was having a hard time getting rid of him again. "I'm just curious, what do you think of Marcus?"

Colleen cocked her head. "Marcus Young? Who works in the bakery?"

"Yes."

A little giggle spilled out of her mouth. "Sorry, I—" she shook her head, "it's just funny. I thought he was this weird spoiled kid who had never had a job and didn't even know how to sweep the floor."

"But?" I sensed she had changed her mind about him.

"But he's turned out to be a hard worker. Fast learner. And he's really good with customers." She shrugged. "All the guests love that British accent."

I flushed thinking about that British accent muttering unmentionable things in my ears as he rammed his cock deep inside me. "Yeah…it's nice to listen to…"

Colleen sighed, but then her businesslike persona returned. She went back to whispering about the details she wanted to discuss.

But, in my mind, I kept replaying that sensation of Marcus's cock sliding into me over and over again.

six

CY

I couldn't believe I actually got to work early. I was never early for anything. Obviously that was some prime grade A pussy if I was willing to get out of bed before seven AM for it.

Jolie must have been running late. I ventured to the arcade on the other side of the castle, thinking I might have time to check the throne room again before heading to the bakery for my shift. The arcade was the place where most of the boys who visited the park hung out while their sisters went to meet The Red Velvet Queen. It was named Gumdrop Galley, which I thought was the lamest possible name for what was supposed to be a cool and adrenaline-fueled hang-out spot for little dudes. I was pretty sure my mother named it. "Gumdrop Galley" had Mom written all over it.

"Hey." I waved to the middle-aged guy with the shaggy dark hair who was arranging prizes in the glass cabinets under the counters. He reminded me a little of Jack Black with his curled-up smirk and sizeable stomach pooch.

"Hey, there. What can I do for you?" He reached his hand across the counter to give me a firm shake.

"Oh, I'm Marcus from the bakery. Just got to work a little early, so I'm checking out the rest of the castle," I lied. "And you are...?"

I could see full well that his nametag read Buster, which had to be a made-up name. *"What a beautiful baby! Let's name him Buster," said no mom ever.*

His lips tilted up as he pointed comically at his nametag. "Buster. And nice to see I'm not the only Brit in Sweetopia!"

Shit.

"What part of the Motherland are you from?" he continued as his gaze swept from my face down my chest and back up again.

I choked out, "Oh, um, just outside London." I cleared my throat and scrambled for the most British thing I could say. "I bloody miss that place!"

His brows furrowed as he continued to examine me. I could tell he was trying to decide whether or not he believed me. "What brings you across the pond?"

"Uni," I said, cranking up the charm. I'd caught a bit of a gay vibe from this Buster dude, and I wasn't above flirting with him just like I did with that Ellie chick in the gift shop.

Whatever it takes, I told myself, images of Greece and twenty-five thousand dollars-worth of cool, crisp Benjamins flying through my mind.

"Studying anything fun?" His gaze swept down me again, and my gaydar was going off louder than ever. *Not that there's anything wrong with it!* my memory echoed with the famous line from *Seinfeld*. My parents fucking loved that show.

"Art history." I offered him a smug smile, knowing this was a topic I could converse on with absolutely no reservations.

"Favorite painter?" His eyebrows quirked, possibly trying to catch me in a lie again.

You couldn't answer this question with something obvious like Monet or Van Gogh. "Bordone," I said with confidence.

"Oh, really? I pegged you for more of a modern bloke." The way he emphasized the word "pegged" did not escape my notice.

"No, definitely not. I prefer the classics. I should have been born during the Renaissance." I wasn't going to let his innuendo distract me from my mission.

Buster's lips curled into a provocative grin. "Yes, I can see that now." The way his eyes traveled up and down my body, it seemed he was appreciating a masterpiece himself.

I could work this to my advantage. Why not just cut to the chase?

"Hey, I was just wondering if you know anything about a secret employee meeting happening next week?"

His grin faded quickly, followed by another blatant brow furrowing. "Who told you about that?" His voice dropped at least an octave.

I shrugged, trying to play it off as naiveté. "I overheard my boss talking about it. I was just wondering where it was so I could attend."

Buster was squinting so hard, his two formerly distinct eyebrows were basically one continuous bushy line across his forehead. "You're a temp, right?"

I nodded. Temps wore a different type of name badge than permanent employees, so he easily ascertained my status.

"We don't typically invite temps to the meetings," Buster said rather flatly.

"Oh." I studied him, wondering how to get back to the

earlier flirty vibe we established so I could glean something useful from this conversation. "Why not?"

"It's not my decision," he answered. "That comes from higher up on the ladder than me."

"Higher up? Who's in charge?" I suspected he noticed the little tremble my voice took on when I realized I was *this close* to figuring out the answer to my undercover mission because his eyes narrowed again.

"I can't give out that type of info, sorry." He reached back down into the glass cabinet to stock more prizes.

"Okay." There was no way I could prevent disappointment from coloring my tone. "Well, do you know who I could talk to about getting more info? I really want to get involved, especially if I try to stay on past the summer."

"Who is your boss?" He scratched at his chin as he eyed me up and down again, just like he had when I'd first introduced myself.

"Colleen Neese," I offered, hoping her name would somehow unlock a secret stash of information Buster didn't seem to want to part with.

"Talk to her," he said.

I wondered if that was a roundabout way of admitting Colleen was the ringleader, the one "higher up on the ladder." I thanked him for his time and ambled back to the bakery, working out in my mind how to confront my boss about the meeting. Again.

COLLEEN ACTUALLY LOOKED SOMEWHAT EXCITED TO SEE ME when I swooped into the bakery while simultaneously tying my apron on. I was glad she was in a good mood because I really needed to pump her for some information.

"Hey there, how goes it?" I squeezed out a charming smile and waited for her to take the bait.

"Good, Marcus, good. How about you? You're certainly looking chipper today." She set down her rolling pin and went to wash her hands in the stainless-steel sink.

"I wanted to ask you something." My pitch lowered to a more serious-sounding level, which made her turn to stare at me.

"Yes?"

"Why don't you allow temps to attend your super-secret meetings?" My head tilted as I looked for her reaction—it might be more telling than her actual words.

"Who told you that?" *Yep, brows arched, eyes wide, lips pursed.* She didn't want to discuss this topic.

"Uh, Buster, the guy at the arcade. He said it wasn't his rule—"

"It's not my rule either," she insisted, drying her hands on a cloth towel. "But I do agree with it. I mean, we want employees there who are invested in the company and who get the health insurance and other benefits. Temps don't."

"Yeah, don't remind me." I shook my head, trying to summon a sad, disappointed tone.

"Why are you so interested in this meeting?" She narrowed her dark eyes on me. "You've brought it up almost every day."

I cleared my throat, buying myself some time to formulate a plausible answer. "Like you said, I'm probably not going to find a job in art history, so I might end up here for a while. I mean, if I can get a full-time position when my temp time is up. So, it seems like company policies might be really important to me here soon. If I can help leverage better pay and benefits in any way, then…I'm all about it." I shot her a confident grin.

She shook her head as she expelled a huff of air. When

she looked at me again, there was kindness in her eyes, a softness that wasn't there moments before. "Marcus, you don't want to work here. You're a sweet kid and all, but I don't know if you're cut out for this place—"

That was a harsh thing for her to say. Especially since I fucking grew up here. How could I not be cut out for my own destiny? Someday I'd be running this park alongside Clem and Carson—once my parents retired, anyway.

She must have sensed the sting her comment inflicted upon me because she was quick to backpedal. "What I mean is that you're a really nice guy. Maybe you're not very experienced, but you have good people skills and a real charming way about you, Marcus. The Sweets—the people who own this place—"

Like I didn't know the Sweets. *For fuck's sake.*

"—they're assholes, Marcus. They don't care about their employees. The benefits suck. The wages suck. Like we were telling you the other day, it's not a family-friendly place, not like you'd think, being a family theme park and all."

"But aren't you trying to change that?" I probed a little deeper, desperately working to stay in character and not defend my parents.

Though, I certainly wanted to. The rant my father would go on if he were listening to this conversation was beginning to rumble up inside me. Didn't he just give me a version of that rant when he was grilling me about this mission in his office the other night?

"A group of us are, yes." I could sense her exasperation as she grabbed some dough out of the fridge and began to pound it against the counter a little more violently than necessary before dusting it with more flour.

I decided to cut to the chase. "Are you in charge of that group?"

Her eyes rocketed to mine in a flash. "No." It was a curt and adamant denial.

I shrugged, trying to play this off as mere curiosity instead of what it really was: an interrogation. "I also heard there's a secret Facebook group for Sweetopia employees. How do you get into that? Or are temps not allowed there either?"

"Did Buster tell you that too?" She huffed out another long breath before rolling the dough out thin and flat against the counter.

"Uh, I can't remember where I heard that one…" I didn't particularly want to implicate anyone I'd conversed with. I needed to protect my sources, and if Colleen was lying about being in charge, she might retaliate against anyone who provided me with information.

"There's a secret group," she confirmed. "But, yes, like the meeting, it's for regular employees only. No temps."

Damn it. I was being thwarted at every turn. I could hear my father's voice ringing in my ear, pushing me to dig deeper, push harder. As if I'd summoned him, the phone began to ring on the other side of the bakery.

Colleen held up her flour-covered hands. "Can you get that?"

"Of course." I nodded to another employee who had raced from the kitchen in the back to help. Then I picked up the old-fashioned landline phone hanging on the tiled wall. "Hello?"

"Oh, hello, Mr. Sweet!" I gushed after hearing my father's voice. "Yes, of course. I will send her right up."

I had suggested that my dad call Colleen up for a meeting so I could snoop around a bit more, but I didn't think he'd really follow through on that. *I guess I was wrong.* I relayed "Mr. Sweet's" message to my boss. Looking completely flustered, Colleen washed her hands before taking off her apron and rushing out the bakery's back door into the secret employee tunnel.

The other bakery employee just looked at me and shrugged. I gave her a polite smile and told her I'd be back in a moment.

I DIDN'T TAKE ME LONG TO REACH THE GIFT SHOP ON THE other side of the castle. It was still early, and there was a long line extending out the throne room, but the gift shop wouldn't be inundated until that line moved past greeting the queen and back into the main hallway. The other place patrons came from was the boat ride dumping its riders off in the gift shop at the end. Genius marketing tactic, of course, creating a captive audience. But the boat ride had just started operating.

Ellie, the manager, wasn't behind the counter, but I soon realized that was a good thing because traffic was already starting to spill in. I flashed a smile like a secret handshake to the employee manning the cash register. I flashed another at the employee out on the floor helping a kid choose a plastic sword, then I let myself into the employees' only area at the back of the store. The light in Ellie's office was on.

"Well, hello there," she oozed, her bright honey-colored eyes shining at me. "You never came back like you said you would."

"Sorry about that." I gave a little shrug. "I'm just now getting a chance. It's been super busy over at the bakery."

"Even this early in the morning?" she questioned, her brows tacking together like she didn't quite believe me. What was with the skepticism among Sweetopia employees? First

Buster didn't buy that I was British or studied art history, and now Ellie was incredulous as well.

"Even this early. Those cookies are addictive! Plus... donuts and coffee, right?" My lips spread into my most charming smile as I prepared to go in for the kill. I wondered what it would cost me: a kiss? A grope?

When Ellie slid out from the desk, my focus snapped to the short, tight skirt she was wearing. It didn't seem like appropriate attire for a children's theme park gift shop manager. She leaned up against her desk, crossing her arms in front of her chest and pushing her small breasts together to form some semblance of cleavage. It was not particularly impressive, especially compared to what The Red Velvet Queen flaunted in her corset. Ellie lowered her gaze, then batted her eyelashes when she glanced up at me, trying desperately to pull off a sexy look. "Trying" being the operative word.

"Still interested in that secret staff meeting?" Her voice was laced with seduction, and she finished her question by shamelessly biting down on her bottom lip.

"Actually, yes." I stepped closer to her, prepared to do whatever it took to gain valuable intel. "Very interested. That's why I came to see you."

Her lips quirked down into a pout. "Is that the only reason?"

I swallowed hard. "Well, I—I'm thinking about taking a full-time job here at the end of the season, and I want to know what to expect...benefits-wise..."

She laughed. "A young, healthy guy like you probably wouldn't have any issues with the health plan here. It's not the best, but...you're single, *right?*" She heavily emphasized the last word, her gaze raking up and down my body.

I nodded and took a small step back. I began to grow

uncomfortable when she closed the distance between us, slipping her arm around my waist.

She was cute, kinda, in a flat-chested sort of way. She had nice eyes and a decent smile.

But she wasn't Jolie.

She wasn't even in the same universe as Jolie.

What on earth was I talking about? I wasn't dating Jolie. We'd fucked in her dressing room, but I'd barely seen her since. I wasn't beholden to her in any way, shape, or form.

I can have my cake and eat it too. What could be "sweeter" than that, pardon the pun?

Besides, confining myself to one woman had never been my thing. I'd never passed up a chance to explore something new, something different, especially when it was so easy, so effortless…being handed to me on a silver platter.

"Why don't you come a little closer?" she purred, grabbing hold of a fistful of my pink polo shirt and pulling me closer to her waiting mouth.

I snapped, jerking back at least three steps. I didn't know who was more surprised by my reaction: me or her.

"You're single, right?" she reiterated, her eyes bouncing between mine in a mixture of embarrassment and desperation.

Fuck. I can't do this.

I had absolutely zero desire to touch this woman or be touched by her.

"Sorry, but—" I stammered as I looked into her eyes, pleading for a second chance, "—but I really just want to know about the meeting. I—"

"You're not gay, are you?" Her brows furrowed as her face froze in a sharp expression of disapproval. Then she shook it away. "Not that there's anything wrong with that."

Maybe she's a Seinfeld fan too? "No, I, uh—"

"Ellie, can you come help this customer? He's trying to

return something, but it's not in the original packaging," came a voice behind me.

Hot damn. Saved by a fellow employee. I knew the girl from the counter wouldn't understand why, but I shot her the most grateful look I could muster before getting the fuck out of there. On my walk back to the bakery, I kept asking myself over and over again what the hell my problem was.

I was so close to getting what I needed, but I couldn't seal the deal.

And it was because of Jolie.

seven

JOLIE

I saw the shadow lurking outside my dressing room door before I realized it was Marcus. He just couldn't stay away, could he?

"Hey, what's up?" His whole face brightened when he saw me unlocking the door.

I turned to my assistant. "You can go. I can finish up in there."

"Are you sure?" Her eyes darted between me and Marcus, seeming unsure about leaving me alone with him. Like she could stop him from harming me if he had a mind to.

Actually, a sick and twisted part of me was wildly curious about what that might look like—him harming me. Brutalizing me with his monster cock. *Mmm, it sounds delicious.*

I patted her on the arm. "Yeah, go on and clock out early. You deserve it."

"Thanks, Your Majesty." She gave me a little curtsy and rushed off down the tunnel toward the park exit.

"Well, Your Majesty, I think we're alone now," Marcus quipped as I pushed my dressing room door open. He didn't hesitate to follow me inside.

I wanted to blow him off. I really needed to get home and not be fucking around with a fellow employee at work, but the look in his eyes was so hungry, so primal, I simply shut the door and turned to face him.

That was all it took. Without another word, he swept me into his arms, and his lips were on mine within a mere heartbeat, tongue probing, fingers digging into the laces of my corset as my lungs squeezed tight in my chest.

"Can't stop thinking about you," he growled into my ear. "I need to be inside you." He took my hand and pressed it to the front of his pants. An impressive bulge strained against the fabric.

"I need to get home—" I started to say.

"I know you don't owe me anything," he said. "If you can't or don't want to, I understand. But I'm going to have to take care of this before I head out. I feel like my balls might explode if I don't come."

Wow, well, that was forward, wasn't it?

"That sounds like a you problem," I quipped, my words edged with mirth.

He tugged me to him, his lips making their way to that spot between my neck and shoulder that made me weak in the knees. Definitely my kryptonite. "Guess I have to convince you it's an us problem," he rasped in a gravelly British accent. "Why don't we make a bet?"

"A bet?" I pulled back and stared at him. "A sexual bet?"

"Yeah." A smirk twisted his lips as his eyes raked up and down my body. "If I can get you off within three minutes, you have to let me come in your pussy."

I looked at the clock on the wall beside the door. "Three

minutes?" The idea of his hands and mouth going to work on my pussy got me halfway there without him even touching me. But three minutes was pretty short...

"C'mon, you know you want to." The lusty glimmer in his eyes sealed the deal.

I huffed out, "Fine."

He wasted no time propping me up against the counter and diving beneath the multiple layers of my dress. The sight of him with voluminous velvet, lace and tulle surrounding him like a cloud was almost funny, but once he stripped my panties down my thighs and his tongue attacked my clit, I no longer found any humor in it. He took my breath away when he thrust two fingers inside me and went to work.

I wasn't watching the clock. I mean, I tried to, but my eyes only stayed open for a few seconds before rolling back in my head when his expert stroke against my G-spot made my juices gush all over his hand. He swallowed them all down, relentlessly licking, sucking and fingering me until I exploded all over his face.

When I looked at the clock again, exactly two and a half minutes had passed.

Fuck!

He didn't say a word, but victory was painted all over his face as he lifted me up, spun me around, and forced me back down again, my elbows resting on the countertop as he settled himself behind me. He pushed my legs farther apart and swatted my bare ass, sending a stinging sensation coursing through my body.

"What was that for?" I snapped over my shoulder.

"Just to remind you I'm in charge now. I won the bet, and now I'm going to have my way with you." He smacked me again for good measure, making another bolt of pleasure rip through me.

"Mmmm, my handprints on your ass are divine. Makes my cock so damn hard…" To corroborate his statement, he slapped his thick, rock-hard shaft against my soft cheek as my juices dripped down my thighs in anticipation.

I wiggled my ass, ready for him, but he was busy sliding a condom into place. He squeezed my cheek hard as he pressed the tip of his cock to my back hole, making me flinch.

"Ever been fucked here?"

My face instantly flushed, but I didn't answer him.

"Jolie?" He pressed the tip into my tight ring of muscles. "Oh, god, you have a virgin ass, don't you?"

I whimpered, "Yes…" I was a little ashamed of that, to be honest. But I'd never had a partner who wanted to explore in that way. I was a dominatrix. I'd pegged plenty of men, but my asshole had never been breached by anything bigger than a tongue or finger.

"Not today…because you need prep…but someday," he promised, "when we have lube and lots more time."

For some reason the thought of him taking his time to lube me up and gently take my anal virginity made me weak in the knees. I'd just come, but desire was already building again just at the prospect of having him inside me—no matter which hole he might choose.

Before I had a chance to contemplate his choice any further, he thrust into my pussy, filling me about halfway before needing to stop and let me adjust to him. Yeah, if he thought he was going to fuck my ass someday, he would need to start preparing me weeks in advance. He was packing some serious heat.

"Oh, god, Jolie, you're so fucking wet and tight. It's not going to take long…but I wanna make you come too," he groaned.

The sensation was so full, so exquisite, his firm grip on

my ass so arousing, all I could do was press back into him, urging him to thrust harder, faster. Any words I wanted to speak were trapped in my throat, and the only thing coming out were raspy breaths and whimpers as he picked up speed.

Now buried to the hilt, he pounded into me, balls slapping against my bare ass. I was glad my dressing room was soundproofed and Sweetopia was understaffed; otherwise, who knew how many of our fellow employees would be listening in on our wild romp?

"Fuck, Jolie, you're gonna make me come," he blurted out, and I braced myself as he relentlessly railed into me. The primal moans erupting from him made my core clench, and I was momentarily suspended before I fell into ecstasy. My orgasm crashed over me as he slowly ground to a halt, collapsing against my corseted back. His dick throbbed and pulsed inside me, draining every last drop of cum from him.

After we cleaned ourselves up, I looked at the clock. From start to finish, this encounter had taken precisely ten minutes.

"Thanks for taking my bet," he said, brushing a lingering kiss to my lips.

I kissed him back. "Well, it was a bet I couldn't lose…"

I THOUGHT MY SESSION WITH THEO WOULD DISTRACT ME FROM everything going on with my son River and his medical treatment, but it turned out, the only thoughts that could distract me from *anything* were the ones about Marcus.

And those weren't exactly welcome.

Not when I was supposed to be tying Theo up and rendering his hiney red as a lobster.

While my hands, mouth, and body were present in the room, cracking the paddle over Theo's backside and clobbering him with a litany of insults and curses (*he really, really likes that shit*), my mind was divided in two. Half was focused on River and the fact that his doctor wanted to admit him to the hospital for a week for what was commonly called a tune-up. I wanted to push it off as long as possible, till the end of summer, if we could, but Dr. Grimes said it wasn't advisable. They wanted to put him on some high-powered antibiotics, a week inpatient and the rest at home. My mom said she would take care of him, but how could I let my baby stay in the hospital and not be there for him?

Summer was the busiest time at Sweetopia. Though my boss, the Director of Characters, claimed to have spoken with the Sweets about my situation a few times, no one seemed to care about me or my son's illness. Last week when I missed a few days, my boss basically said that I had better not miss any more time this summer. That was why putting River's tune-up off till fall would work so much better.

There would be smaller crowds and reduced hours at the park, and it would be much easier for me to get away. Not to mention, if we were able to get the Sweets to re-evaluate their health plan and leave policy after the strike we were organizing, I would hopefully be in a better position to pay the hospital bills and take time off.

In any case, the guilt just fucking stabbed me, twisting a knife right into my back.

I was drowning in guilt most days. How could I have given my precious son this disease? His father and I were both carriers, apparently—not that his father even stuck around to see him born.

I tried to find him once upon a time, shortly after River's diagnosis. I planned to sue him for support. The asshole signed away his rights, saying he never wanted to be contacted again. What kind of man abandoned his own son? Especially one who was sick? Only a true monster.

No wonder I'd let the other half of my mind drift to Marcus again and again. Yes, he was young and just a temp worker—he could never be a partner for me or a father figure for my sons. I didn't even want anyone in that role, no matter how much my mother insisted I needed someone to fill it.

But Marcus was fun. The time I spent with him, I was able to forget, for just a moment, how royally sucktastic my life was, pardon the pun. I deserved a few moments of fun in my life, didn't I?

I saw Marcus earlier today right before I left. He was on break and came to see if I was on break too. Of course, I wasn't. So he just stood at the back of the throne room and made faces at me, trying to get me to break character. *Silly boy.*

Somehow I managed to preserve my queenly countenance. It took every drop of strength I had, though. No wonder I didn't have the concentration I needed for Theo tonight.

"Mistress Magenta?" Theo's small voice came muffled from behind the latex mask he was wearing.

I bent down to look my sub in the eyes. He usually took his punishment without comment, so I was worried I'd gone too hard on him. "Yes?"

"May I use the restroom?" he asked, his voice quivering.

"Yes. Go ahead." I unhooked his collar from where he was tethered to the bench we were playing on. Ordinarily, I would have made him do something for me in exchange for the freedom to go piss, but I was obviously off my game tonight. And I needed to wrap up this session. I rented a space in a dungeon, and it was scheduled for another session with a different dominatrix at the top of the hour.

I didn't feel like I'd given my all today as either Mom, Queen, or Domme. I'd let too many thoughts of Marcus and his mouthwatering cock seep in.

I pledged to do better tomorrow.

eight

JOLIE

My vow to do better was quickly forgotten when I found Marcus waiting outside my dressing room the next morning. He wasn't wearing his Sweetopia logo shirt yet, but rather a charcoal-gray tank top that showed off his arm muscles. How could he be totally ripped and be a nerd too? It just defied logic that someone like him, the perfect dichotomy of brains and brawn, could exist.

"What's up?" rolled off his tongue as he pushed off the wall to lean toward me for a peck on the lips. "I feel like I've barely seen you in the past week."

I bristled when his lips hit mine. I knew there were cameras in this hallway and hoped he'd get the hint when I flashed my gaze up at the one aimed directly at us. I dug my keys out of my purse and quickly unlocked the door. There were no cameras in my dressing room. Thank god.

"Sorry." I gestured to the rolling chair in the corner my makeup artist used when she worked on me. A glance at the clock above my mirror warned that she'd be arriving in only ten minutes. I had some makeup on, but she would do my eyes and lips, then come back at lunchtime to touch them up after I ate.

"I've never seen you without all your makeup on," Marcus observed as he rolled the chair close to me.

"Sorry to disappoint you. The eyelashes are fake." I arranged my gown around my thighs as I took a seat, the boning of my corset digging into my ribcage. I must have put on a few pounds in the last couple weeks. My costume seemed tighter than normal. *Stress eating,* I realized. *Because of River.*

"Whatever," he retorted, his dark eyes shining, "you look beautiful just the way you are." He ran a finger down my arm and then took my hand into his.

"I bet you wouldn't say that if you saw me out of costume," I snapped back. Then I instantly regretted it. Because he might want to.

"What, are you like hiding a third leg under there or something?" His lips turned up into a soft smile. "I've pretty much seen what you've got, Jolie. Maybe not all at once, but I've seen enough to know you're stunning, in or out of costume. You are a fucking work of art—and I should know, I've studied plenty of art."

I desperately fought off a blush that wanted to creep out from behind my ears and across my cheeks. *What the fuck is this? I don't blush.* How could I be falling for all his lame lines and cheesy attempts at flirtation? The accent must lower my defenses or something. Or maybe it was the combo of the glasses and the scruffy beard.

Then again, knowing he could back up those cheesy lines with that massive cock he harbored between his legs was probably a major contributing factor. Just watching the way his eyes trailed down my arms, across my cleavage, and then back up to my face was making my nipples hard. I wanted his hands on me, his lips. I wanted him to have his way with me again like he did a few days ago. I had thought of nothing else —even though I knew it was wrong for me to obsess. *So wrong.*

"So what are you doing here this morning, Marcus?" I struggled to keep my voice even, smooth. My chest was heaving under his thick, hard stare, knowing he was working hard to refrain from touching me. How badly I wished his restraint would fail.

"I wanted to see you," he answered without hesitation. "Like I said, I missed you most of the week. Is everything okay?"

I gulped. Did he really want to know if things were okay? Because they sure as fuck weren't.

Things were pretty fucking far from okay, in fact. Everything was a mess, between River's medical issues and Reed having some problems at school. Between my two damn jobs and the Sweets offering the fucking worst health insurance on the planet. Sometimes I wondered if I'd be better off not even working and trying to get government assistance.

But no, I had to prove something. I had to prove that a single mom could do shit herself. That she didn't need a man to take care of her.

And I was proving that, right? I was sitting on a fucking throne, after all. What more could I want? I was torn between feeling ungrateful for what I had achieved and wanting more, more, more.

"Jolie?" When he said my name, he gripped my hand in his, and there was true concern etched into just those two short syllables. He said it like a French speaker would, with a "jzho" at the beginning. It was the way my mother pronounced it. Most other people I knew said it with a regular "J" sound, like "Joe-lee." The way it came off Marcus's lips made it sound like the most beautiful word in the universe.

"I'm sorry." I glanced back up from my hand, which looked so small and delicate in his, to his eyes. "I just have a lot going on. My makeup artist is going to be here any minute to finish me up."

"Right." He squeezed my hand again. "I just...wanted to spend a little time with you."

He was the sweetest guy. No wonder I was feeling butter-flies. It wasn't just because of his ridiculous skills, but because of that deep, soft voice, that look in his eyes...that look that almost asked if he could take care of me.

Like I need someone to take care of me!

I straightened up, feeling the boning in my corset dig in as I filled my lungs with all the air they could hold. "Maybe we can catch up later?"

His fingertips grazed across the thick velvet fabric of my dress before his hands flew to my waist. Next thing I knew, he was pulling me onto his lap, the material of my dress swallowing up his thighs until I was solidly perched upon him.

My heart raced as his fresh, clean, masculine scent filled my senses. "What are you doing?"

He didn't answer, just used his finger to tilt my chin toward his before claiming my lips with his own. He hungrily sucked my bottom lip between his teeth before his tongue delved into my mouth, parting my lips in conquest. I swooned in his embrace, and when I caught myself and tried to straighten back up, his grip around my waist only tight-ened, forcing me to succumb to his advances.

The problem was, succumbing was all I wanted to do. I couldn't fight him off. Yes, I could have pushed him off phys-ically—that was not the issue. I simply could not will myself to do so. His draw was too powerful, his lips too entrancing.

The knock came loudly on the door, almost a pounding, and my heart leapt in my chest, taking off at a gallop as though it might just burst right through my ribs and corset. "Oh, shit. You've gotta go."

I jumped off his lap, amused by how disoriented he was, like he was still lost in the moment of kissing me. It took him several seconds to recover before he stood up, and there was no way he could hide his extremely visible erection making a huge tent in his khaki pants. He pulled his uniform polo out of his back pocket, where apparently the tail of it had been tucked. I hadn't even noticed; I was too busy staring at his bare arms.

He smirked as he pulled it over his head, and, fortunately, it was long enough to cover up his arousal. The pounding at the door came again, followed by my assistant yelling, "Jolie? Jolie, you in there?"

"She walked in on me naked once, and now, even though she has a key, she always makes sure I'm dressed first." As soon as I said it, I realized how frightening it made my naked body seem. And reminded me that this thing with Marcus could never go past secret trysts in my dressing room.

He just laughed, like he didn't believe a word I was saying. "Can I come back after our shift? Please? I want to do that thing again—"

My eyebrows arched. "'That thing?'"

"What I did the first time I was in here…" His voice trailed off as if he couldn't quite get the words out.

Isn't that adorable? He couldn't just say he wanted to go down on me.

I should say no. I should say hell *no.*

I didn't have a dominatrix session after work, but I did need to get home to get River packed up for the hospital. My mother was taking him in the morning.

"I really can't, Marcus…"

"Just fifteen minutes," he pleaded. "Just give me fifteen minutes, and I promise you won't regret it."

I couldn't prevent a smile from lifting the corners of my mouth, but I added an eye roll as my sole defense. "Alright, fine. But fifteen minutes tops."

He leaned in to kiss me on the cheek. "I'll see you at five, then."

CY

I had some intel to gather before meeting Jolie back in her dressing room at five, but Colleen was getting suspicious of all my bathroom breaks.

Her head cocked like she was trying to figure me out. "So, are you a smoker or something?"

"What? No," I fired back, not able to hide my offense.

"IBS?" she guessed again.

"Huh?" I stared at her, no idea what she was talking about.

"Irritable Bowel Syndrome," she enunciated in a whisper.

"Eww, no." Though, now that I thought about it, going along with that would probably garner me a free hall pass for the rest of the summer. I could just say my bowels were on fire and in danger of erupting. Like Mount Vesuvius or something. But, no, I didn't want to go there.

"I'm just trying to figure out why you're disappearing every few minutes, Marcus. Can you help me out here?" Her brown eyes were wide with a mixture of concern and frustration.

"Sorry, I've just been trying to find out more about this meeting happening next week. Everyone's been so hush-hush. I'm trying to assimilate and infiltrate the Sweetopia culture, and you're all shutting me down at every turn." I crossed my arms over my chest as though I were really flummoxed about the whole thing. Maybe I could push her empathy buttons?

"Why do you want to do that so bad?" she pushed, and I felt the strong possibility of another anti-Sweetopia rant bubbling to the surface.

"I know you said this is a shitty—ahem, I mean, 'bad' place to work—" I glanced around to see if any children or, even worse, mothers heard my curse word. Fortunately, the bakery was rather empty. It was our post-lunch slump. Things would pick up again in another hour or so as kids burned off their lunches and needed more sugar to jack up their energy levels.

"I didn't say that exactly, Marcus." Her jaw clenched a bit tighter with each word. "I said that the Sweets have some morale issues, and it's mostly because Corden Sweet is up there in his gold-plated office counting his billions while many of his workers struggle to pay their bills and feed their families."

"But you do okay as a manager, right?" I pushed back. "It's my understanding that most of the employees here are either retirees or students. Their incomes are subsidized by social security or by their parents. They don't have families to feed."

She rolled her eyes. "Seriously? Marcus, *you* may be a student, and you may still be sucking at your parents' teats, but look around. Take off the rose-colored glasses. There are plenty of park employees with families. What about your friend Jolie, for example?"

I froze. I hadn't ever asked her about her family situation.

Taking in my bewildered expression, my boss looked like she was on the verge of having a laughing fit at my expense. "Oh, don't look at me like that. I know you're sweet on her.

Don't even try to deny it. The way you look at her when she comes in here in the morning doesn't hide a thing."

Okay, whatever, so she knows I have a thing for Jolie. It's a free country.

"So, what about Jolie?" I tried to downplay the crush she was accusing me of having.

"She's a single mom," Colleen explained in a tone that made it clear she thought I should have already known.

"Really?" That was the only word I could muster. I felt like the air had been knocked out of my lungs. She never mentioned having a child…then again, I didn't exactly ask. *And I'm not sure that's something you bring up when a dude is fucking you in your dressing room at work.*

"Hey, Colleen, is the coffee fresh?" came a familiar voice from the bakery entrance. It was Buster from the arcade. He was carrying an aluminum coffee mug with a hot pink Sweetopia logo, the kind of mug we offered for discounted refills. "I come seeking a caffeine hit." He fluttered his eyelashes at her and set the mug on the counter.

"I can get it," I offered. I needed to stay on his good side, even if it meant enduring his relentless flirting. He was nowhere near as bad as Ellie in the gift shop.

When I turned around to fill up the mug, Colleen picked up our conversation right where we'd left off, apparently inviting Buster to weigh in. "So, Mr. Young here doesn't think Sweetopia employees have it that bad when it comes to compensation and benefits," she filled him in, "because he doesn't think we're supporting families."

"Is that so?" Buster's voice rose a whole octave while he waited, bouncing on one foot and then the other, for his afternoon hit.

"I just said that most of the park's employees' are either dependents of their parents or they collect social security." It was no secret that the geriatric demographic was well represented among the staff. Employing so many senior citizens was actually something my parents prided themselves upon. Hell, they were getting pretty far up there in age themselves. No wonder they felt an obligation to help seniors out.

"That's bullshit," Buster didn't mince words. "There are a lot of young parents here. I have a daughter myself."

My eyes bugged out before I could stop them. "Really?" I exclaimed for the second time that day. How could Buster and Jolie both be...parents? The concept was so foreign to me.

Buster nodded. "Yup. Didn't you ever read *And Tango Makes Three* when you were growing up?" He laughed and dramatically flicked his wrist in the air. "Of course, her father and I are now divorced. We have joint custody, but that makes me a single dad." He struck a theatrical pose. "A devastatingly handsome gay single dad."

"See?" Colleen whipped around with an artfully decorated dragon cookie sealed in a clear plastic bag that she handed to Buster. He in turn presented her with a sparkling grin and a deep, appreciative bow.

I wanted to tell them that I'd seen the staff demographics. I'd seen how much my parents spent on the payroll and on health insurance and other benefits. It was a shit ton of money. But, naturally, I couldn't divulge any of that in my undercover role.

I was suddenly tired of debating all of this labor bullshit. I just wanted five o'clock to get here so I could go fuck Jolie. Forget this fucking undercover assignment. My parents should have sent one of my brothers. I was not the right person for this job. Clearly.

All I could think about was Jolie naked and writhing beneath me as I brought her to climax again and again and again.

"There's also someone on staff who has a terminally ill

kid," Buster continued, wrangling my attention away from the fantasy it was creating starring one exquisite Red Velvet Queen. I was undoing the clasps on her corset and—

"Shhh," Colleen warned, shooting Buster a glare. "I know the person you're speaking of, and that person would want his or her privacy respected, you know?"

"It's going to come out soon enough." Buster ignored my boss's admonishment. "The employee in question is having a hard time paying for medical treatment for their sick kid, and they've been in contact with the local media. A story is going to break really soon, not long after the meeting."

My ears perked up. *Oh, the meeting. This conversation may be fruitful, after all.* "So, why not just let me come to the meeting, and I can see for myself how bad the situation is?"

"The meeting is for full-time Sweetopia employees," Buster reminded me. "Not temps."

Why did my parents decide to make me a seasonal worker? Obviously, it was their mistake, and it was costing me vital intel. If I couldn't complete this mission, it wouldn't be my fault.

I shot Colleen a look that wasn't too far off from Buster's cajoling caffeine plea mere moments ago. At least I was putting in a valiant effort. When I wasn't daydreaming about fucking Jolie.

"I still don't know why you're so keen on getting a full-time position here," she said with a sigh. "I mean, you didn't even know how to use a mop two weeks ago. And now all the sudden you like manual labor?"

"I feel like I have what it takes for advancement." I flashed her my trademark smile and adjusted my glasses on my face. Yup, I was going to advance right into the corporate offices after this little undercover mission, and my trip to Greece, with an office right between Clem and Carson's. "Plus, I want to stay in the States. As long as I'm working, I should be able to stay here…"

"What, you think you're going to marry The Red Velvet Queen, get your Green Card and ride off into the sunset?" Colleen asked with a chuckle. Buster clearly saw the amusement too and burst into raucous laughter. "You really do belong in a fairy-tale theme park!"

"Just let me come to the meeting," I brought the conversation full circle. "If this place sucks that bad, then fine. I don't know why you're so adamant I not work here…"

"We're just trying to save you from a lifetime of misery," Buster retorted, then glanced over at Colleen for confirmation. She hung her head a bit and nodded. All her earlier mirth had vanished.

"I thought you said it wasn't that bad." My parents weren't going to be too happy when they heard about this discussion.

"Let me check with a few people." Colleen's gaze traveled to the entrance of the bakery, where a family was headed inside as soon as they figured out how to maneuver their double stroller through the door. "If they say it's okay, I'll give you the location."

My smile brightened. I was finally getting somewhere.

nine

CY

"Hello, beautiful!" I tapped on the edge of her dressing room door before letting myself inside. Jolie had collapsed in the dark green wingback chair in the corner of the room, her face buried in her hands. A mess of black curls covered her like a veil. The contrast of her red velvet dress and the green chair made her look like she was posing for a Christmas card.

"What's wrong?" I headed in her direction, noting how my heart took a swift dive toward the bottom of my gut when I saw her frazzled appearance.

She glanced up at me, her usually glittering eyes looking dull, tired. "Sorry, I forgot you were coming." She straightened herself in the chair and appeared to force a smile. It wasn't the kind that made her eyes crinkle that I was used to seeing. "You've got fifteen minutes."

I shook my head as I stopped directly in front of her chair and crouched down to meet her face to face. "No, forget that.

What's wrong, Jolie? Why don't you change out of your costume?"

She echoed my headshake. "The Sweets insist I stay in full costume any time I'm in the park. They don't want any guests to see me partially in costume. They think it would be confusing for my little fans. Sometimes I cheat because I'm running late, but most of the time I get dressed and put on my wig at home. I do most of my makeup there, and then the makeup artist finishes the rest when I get here—"

"Wig?" That was the only word I was able to grab on to. "That's a wig?"

She squinted at me, her brows almost meeting as she let out a huff and ran her fingers through her raven curls. "You thought this was real?"

I shrugged. Well, I'd hoped it was. "So, what does your real hair look like?"

She stood and crossed to the other side of the room, putting her curvy backside on display. If I wasn't mistaken, she was wringing her hands in front of her. I was getting such a stressed-out vibe from her that it was beginning to put me on edge too.

I wasn't used to people's emotions bleeding over into my own. Normally, I didn't give a single fuck how other people felt as long as they weren't interfering with me. But the distress radiating off her was leaving me with a sick feeling deep in my gut, a new and entirely unwelcome sensation.

All I could think was that I truly wanted to help her.

But I didn't know how to go about it. Wanting to help anyone was a totally new thing for me. I was a virgin when it came to helping people.

"Jolie?" I pressed. "Talk to me, please?"

Please? I didn't beg people to talk to me, especially not women. What the hell was going on with me? It was like an alien from Planet Give a Fuck had taken over my mouth, my brain. *Totally unacceptable.*

When she turned around, she wore a muddled expression on her face. It looked like a mixture of regret and disappointment.

"I can't do this, Marcus," she said, her voice low and even. "I'm just not the person you think I am—"

"Because that's not your real hair?" I laughed as I reached out for her hand. She was worried *she* wasn't the person *I* thought she was? I was *definitely* not the person *she* thought *I* was.

She backed away, folding her arms across her chest, but she couldn't cover the ample cleavage spilling out the top of her corset. Truth be told, I was less interested in that than how I could make her smile again.

What the actual fuck? I, Cy Sweet, was more interested in a woman's smile than her tits?

This was a fucking momentous occasion right here. Like Neil Armstrong walking on the moon or, you know, the *alien usurping my brain* theory I shared moments ago. Either way, there was some serious space shit going down right now.

"I'm not really The Red Velvet Queen, you know," she revealed with the start of a smile, though her tone had a slight patronizing tint to it.

I couldn't help but laugh again. "Uh, duh, I'm well aware of that." *I'm not Marcus Young, either,* I wanted to add, but, of course, I couldn't blow my cover.

"You might not like the person I am out of this costume." She fixed her amethyst gaze on me, testing me.

"You mean the fact that you're a mom?" Well, I wasn't planning to let that slip, but now that it was out there, it wasn't exactly like I could take it back...

Her eyes widened as they bounced between mine. "How did you know that?"

"Colleen told me." I tried reaching for her again. "Please? Let me touch you."

She relented this time, letting one hand fall into mine. Her skin was cool to the touch, so I warmed it against my own, rubbing slightly. She let out a soft sigh, her eyes half-closed before they bolted open and locked with mine.

"I don't understand what you want from me, Marcus." Her voice sounded small, defeated, not the royal voice I'd heard her use in the throne room.

I'd had a few girls corner me about "what I wanted." I made it pretty clear what I wanted when I whipped out my sizeable assets. There was usually a pretty swift under-standing that developed between myself and any ladies I might fancy.

But Jolie was not a girl. She was a woman. And the jumble of thoughts and, dare I say it, *feelings* bombarding me right now was making me say weird things, foreign things. And it wasn't just because of my fake accent.

"Nothing in particular." I squeezed her hand in mine and held her gaze captive with my own. "Except maybe a date?"

"A date?" The quizzical way her mouth formed an O and her eyebrows arched made me guess that perhaps she hadn't had one of those in a long time.

"Yeah," I confirmed. "To get to know the real Jolie. The one under the costume."

"I still don't know—"

My finger instinctively went to her lips to stop her from finishing her sentence.

She backed away, wrangling her hand out from my grasp. "It doesn't bother you that I'm older? That I have children?"

"Children?" I gulped. "Plural?"

I still didn't understand why people wanted to make miniature versions of themselves.

She rolled her eyes. "Yes. I have two sons."

"Wow," I breathed out, trying to conceal my shock. *Well, if you pop out one kid, you might as well pop out another, right? My parents popped out three, after all, and they're smart, reasonable people. Well, they're smart anyway.*

"That's great," I quickly recovered, letting the alien in my head take over again. "I don't think you're that much older than me, anyway. What are you doing tomorrow night?"

"I have to think about it." Her features had softened. There was a spark dancing in her pupils again.

Well, it wasn't a no. That was something at least.

"Think about it?" I repeated. "Okay." I wasn't used to ladies needing to *think about it* where I was concerned. *This conversation is just full of firsts, isn't it?*

"I have to see if I can get a sitter...you know..." She fluttered her hand in front of her face as if that would finish the rest of her sentence.

No, I didn't know how these things worked. I was the youngest of the three sons in my family, and none of us had kids yet—much to my parents' dismay. But, so far, Carson bore the biggest brunt of that complaint, by virtue of being the only one of us who was married.

"If not tomorrow night, then maybe Saturday night?" I regretted the hopeful upswing of my voice, but there was no way to hide my anticipation. "Or...I'm free all next week."

I mean, I was pretty much free every night until I left for Greece. And I really wanted to have my way with her a few more times before I went. She made this undercover gig tolerable.

Though, in all honesty, I did kind of like Colleen and some of my other coworkers too. *Damn it. Did I actually just admit that?*

"Next week is the meeting." She looked me up and down. "You're not just trying to get an invite to the secret meeting, are you?"

I chuckled as I shook my head. "I already got one. Colleen is checking on it for me."

Jolie's eyes narrowed. "Mmmhmmm," was all she said.

"Here, let me give you my number," I suggested, my eyes trailing over to the phone on her vanity. "Is that yours?"

She nodded, reaching for it. "Okay." She paused, waiting for me to rattle off my digits.

I much preferred having her number than giving my own, so I whipped my phone out. "Let me text it to you."

"Uh, wrong. Give me the number, Romeo," she snapped with a smirk. She was clearly on to me.

After I gave it to her, she laid her phone back on the counter and turned to me. "I'm still not sure about going on a date with you. I don't know if you'll still like me once you see who I am under all this." She gestured from her wig all the way down to her velvet slippers, which just barely peeked out from the hem of her dress.

"If that's what you're afraid of," I took her hand again, "don't be. I know you're just as beautiful underneath that costume as you are…well, you know what I'm trying to say." I laughed, unable to finish the compliment I was trying to deliver. *Real smooth. Fuck.*

In lieu of flubbing up my words again, I swept her into my arms, claiming her lips with my own. How perfectly she fit into my embrace, how sweet her mouth tasted. It was so magical and yet so natural at the same time.

I released her moments later and watched her spin back down to earth after our breathtaking kiss. There was no way she wasn't just as beautiful underneath that costume.

There was only one slight problem: I was basically in costume too. I had no choice but to take her on our date as Marcus Young. I couldn't blow my cover when I was so close to victory.

She basically hated my family. How angry would she be when she discovered I was actually Cy Sweet?

THE BEST TIME TO SHOW UP UNANNOUNCED AT MY PARENTS' house was dinnertime. Maureen's cooking was about nine million times better than my own. Who am I kidding? I didn't really cook so much as heat stuff up in the microwave —or order takeout. Now *that* I was rather accomplished at.

"How's my baby?" my mom gushed as soon as I rounded the corner into the living room. My parents were both stretched out on opposite sofas, my mom with her reading glasses and a book and my father with the remote control in his clutches.

I proceeded directly to my mother to bend down and let her give me the obligatory greeting kiss on my cheek. I let her think I was a Mama's boy. It always worked to my advantage.

"Hi, Mom, I'm fine," I greeted her. "Hey, Dad."

My dad relinquished the remote control, setting it on the marble-topped end table, but he left some program about the stock market blaring in the background. "What's going on? Did you figure out where the meeting is on Monday night?"

"How did you know it's on Monday night?" I glared at him. Why was I doing all this recon work if he already knew this shit? I hadn't even gotten the actual date confirmed yet.

"My PR guy has a mole in the secret Facebook group," he explained, "but they won't give out any of the meeting details, time or location, till the last minute. Supposedly it's to keep it on the downlow." He rolled his eyes and shook his head. "Imagine your own employees holding a meeting on your own damn property to bitch about you!"

"Who's to say it's in the park?" I hadn't really thought of that before. If it was held in a public place, how could they keep anyone they didn't want there out?

"Corden, calm down. Dinner is going to be ready in a moment, and you know you'll lose your appetite if you get too irate," my mom piped up, shooting my dad a warning glare.

He completely ignored my mother and turned toward me. "They are meeting to finalize their media campaign." He pinched the bridge of his nose as though it hurt him to relay the details to me. "I am afraid they are going to strike, Cy. I need you to stop this meeting. Stop the media from finding out."

"I don't know how to do that, Dad." At this point, I was getting close to telling him to get Clem or Carson to take over. I was sick of all this sneaking around, not to mention betraying the trust of the friends I'd made like Jolie, Colleen, Buster and a few other bakery employees.

"Cy," my mother took over, taking a cue from the red, angry rage spreading across my father's cheeks. He looked as though he was going to blow a gasket at any moment.

"What, Mom? I'm doing the best I can, for fuck's sake!" I snapped at her.

"Don't you dare use that language to speak to your mother!" my dad berated me. "You are skating on thin ice, Son. If you can't find out who is organizing this effort and stop them from going to the media—and keep them from striking and interfering with park operations—then you can kiss your inheritance goodbye. You can kiss *all* our support goodbye, in fact."

"What? You can't do that, Dad. That's not fair!" I protested, glancing back and forth between him and my mother, hoping at least she would be on my side.

"Cy, we've been trying to get you to grow up and take

responsibility for your future for years," my mother said in her soft yet still completely patronizing voice. "We've given you this mission as a way of proving that you're a real adult, and that you're committed to helping your brothers run Sweetopia after we retire. We are getting up there in age, darling. We need our three sons to step up and fill our shoes—and soon. We would like to retire after the next summer season."

My eyebrows shot up into my hairline. "Next summer? Why so soon?"

"Your dad's health isn't in the best shape. His doctor thinks it's time for him to retire. He's under too much stress," she explained.

I looked over at Dad, but he just stared at the television like he wasn't listening to her talk about him. Then, just when I thought he wasn't paying attention, he whipped his head around to face me.

"Your brother has been doing some surveillance of his own," he shared. "And it's become clear you've befriended one of my employees…a woman by the name of Jolie Cox. Is that true?"

Fuck. No one was supposed to know that. Except Colleen, but she only figured it out because she could read it all over me when Jolie was around.

"Yeah, so?" I didn't like where this was going. I could just tell I wasn't going to like it.

"Well, there is considerable evidence that she is involved in this employee uprising," my dad continued. "If you were doing your job like we asked, you would have already known that."

I rolled my eyes. "I know she's planning to go to the meeting, but I don't think she's involved in the organization."

"What about your boss, Colleen Neese?" my mom fired at me.

My jaw clenched as I struggled to keep my volume from rising defensively. "She's planning to attend, but, again, I don't think she's in charge. She said she had to check with some other people to see if she can offer me an invitation. To me, that means she doesn't know or have the authority to approve my attendance herself. I'm trying to get the details so I can be there, Dad. And I will record it."

"It's probably a cover-up," my mom theorized. "I told you when you promoted Colleen to management she was going to be a problem." She shook her head and let out a deep sigh. "But do you ever listen to me?"

"We've got Ms. Cox on camera passing notes to some other employees in the hallways of the castle, and her assistant has delivered some notes to her on the throne. The throne room is full of cameras, as you know, as are the hallways and tunnels," my father continued, once again not bothering to acknowledge my mother.

"So what?" I could no longer hide my exasperation. "Why is nothing I do ever good enough for you two? I just said I'm going to infiltrate the meeting. What the hell else am I supposed to do?"

"You have a relationship with Ms. Cox," my dad fired back, his voice now lowering to the same level I always heard him use with William and with his executive staff at work. It was his business tone. If it came out, it meant you were expected to comply with his wishes. No ifs, ands, or buts. "You need to leverage that to stop the organizers from going to the media. And you need to make sure the employees don't strike."

My head was starting to pound, the beginnings of a headache hammering away at my temples as my frustration rose. "How do you expect me to pull that off? I'm just a summer temp. I have no fucking power."

"Cyrus Anthony Sweet!" my mother gasped. "Quit

stressing your father out and do as you're told. If you can't handle this assignment, then there won't be a Sweetopia for you and your brothers to inherit. Do you understand?"

I simply nodded, turned on my heel and marched toward the front door. I had suddenly lost my appetite. I tried not to slam the door behind me, but it was still a little slammy, despite my best efforts.

I got in my stupid beat-up truck that I couldn't wait to quit driving, consoling myself with the fact that my trip to Greece was only a week away. I couldn't wait to bask in paradise, soak in the Santorini sunshine and feel the warm waters of the Aegean Sea gently lap at my feet.

If only I could take Jolie with me. Then I would be looking forward to it even more. Then it truly would be paradise.

ten

"So do you want to go out with him?" my mom pressed as we cleaned up the dishes from dinner. The house was so quiet without River there. Reed was in his room doing homework. I'd stopped by the hospital after work, and Mom was going to run over there while I got Reed ready for bed and tucked in. Then I would go and spend the night with River on the tiny fold-out sofa in his cramped room.

"I don't know, Mom. He's so much younger than me." It was the handiest excuse I could think of. I'd been thinking about Marcus asking me out on a date ever since he left my dressing room two and a half hours ago, and I had a feeling the topic was going to haunt my dreams all night as well.

My mom's brows quirked. "How much younger?"

"Six years, I think? He has a degree in art history," I filled her in.

"Art history?" Her nose wrinkled up. "What is he going to do with that?"

"Work at Sweetopia?" I joked. "Did I mention he's British?"

"British! Does he have an accent?" My mom put her hand to her chest as though she was experiencing a swoon. Though it could have been a hot flash. She'd had a lot of those lately.

I nodded. "Yeah, and he wears *glasses.*"

"Jolie, he sounds like your dream man!" My mother giggled as she laid a hand on my shoulder. "Is he nice? Gentlemanly?"

I had to chuckle. She seemed as taken with Marcus as I was, and she hadn't even met him. She was generally quite skeptical about any man who showed an interest in me. She had been since Reed's father broke our engagement after learning I was pregnant and planned to carry the baby. He wanted me to have an abortion.

I'd always pictured myself as a mom. My own mother had always been my best friend, and when my father passed away around the time River was born, my mother needed me as much as I needed her. That was when she moved in, and we'd been roommates ever since. I didn't know what I would do without her. She was my rock. All I knew growing up was that I wanted to be that rock for my own children.

So when I got pregnant with Reed, even though I was young, I knew I could handle it. I'd learned from the best. I just figured Robbie, his dad, and I would get married a little earlier than we expected. I never thought he'd abandon me.

And then a few years later, Tim, River's father, walked out of my life too. Except I knew that one wouldn't last. He was a "rock star"—in that he had a band, and he drank too much. But he wore glasses and had that intellectual side I'd always been attracted to. The rock star persona didn't do a damn thing for me, but the fact that he quoted Walt Whitman to me on our first date? That got him in my pants.

"I think you should go," my mother decided, drying her hands on the dish towel before tossing it on the counter. "When was the last time you went out and had fun?"

"Um, is that a rhetorical question?" I narrowed my eyes at her. She knew damn well I hadn't been out since River was diagnosed with cystic fibrosis three years ago. I had a couple of girlfriends I hung out with before that, but then I ended up having to leave that job because the health insurance was even worse than what they offered at Sweetopia. I'd lost touch with those girls, and, since then, I hadn't made any girlfriends my own age. The closest was Colleen at work, and she had to be at least ten years older than me.

"I'm serious, Jolie. You need a few hours off. You work sixty hours a week. You Mom twenty-four/seven/three hundred sixty-five. Everyone needs a break," my mother said. "And when one gets an opportunity to go on a date with a hot British nerd with glasses, one does not say no!"

"Hmm, words to live by," I teased her.

"They are important words! They oughta be on a t-shirt or something!" My mother laughed and put her arm around my shoulder. "So how about this: you stop by and see River after work tomorrow, then go on your date. I'll stay here with Reed until you get home, then I'll go spend the night with River. You shouldn't have to sleep on that blasted fold-out more than one night anyway."

Tears burned at the corners of my eyes. "Oh, Mom, I can't ask you to do that!"

"You're not asking. I'm insisting." She set her lips in a firm, straight line. "And that's the way it's going to be. *Capiche?*"

Her Italian was coming out. She was Italian on her mother's side and a mix of German, British and Native American on her dad's. But it was always the Italian that came out when she set her mind to something. She always said her mother was the most stubborn woman in the world. I didn't remember my grandmother that well, but it was hard to imagine her being any more stubborn than my mother.

"Fine, Mom," I conceded, watching her face light up with an excited smile. She was truly happy for me, and it was the first time I'd seen that expression on her face in a long time.

I finished up with Reed, getting him all ready for bed before heading out to my car so I could drive to the hospital. The night sky was glittering with a million stars, and I couldn't help but pick out a few constellations as I settled myself behind the wheel. The Big Dipper. Cassiopeia, the latter one notable since she was a queen, and so was I. At least I played one during work hours.

I took out my phone and pulled up the number I'd put in for Marcus. I took a deep breath and composed a text.

> Me: Did you see the stars tonight?

Much to my surprise, he texted back immediately.

> Marcus: Good evening, my Queen.

I nearly swooned just from that alone.
And then:

> Marcus: I did see the stars. There's a nice
> view of Cygnus the Swan tonight.

Holy shit, he knew astronomy too.

> Me: Turns out I'm free tomorrow night.

> Marcus: Me too. Whatever should we do?

> Me: Hey, you're the one who asked me out!

Marcus: I will think of something. What time?

Me: Seven?

Marcus: Perfect. Can I pick you up?

Me: Just give me an address.

Marcus: I will. See you tomorrow, Your Royal Highness.

Me: I told you, I won't look like a queen without my costume.

Marcus: You'll always be a queen to me.

eleven

JOLIE

I pulled up to the address Marcus left for me. It was a really nice area of Naples, but then again, there were a *lot* of nice areas in Naples. Lots of rich people lived here. I wouldn't be living here at all if it wasn't where Sweetopia was located. We were in Fort Myers before, back when I worked at Barney's.

It got depressing sometimes to drive around and look at all the oceanfront mansions. It always made me wonder what I did wrong in life to end up on the other side of the tracks as a single mom supporting three other people working two shitty jobs. Did I royally fuck up somewhere along the way? Did I not suck the right dick? Maybe I just needed to march myself up to Mr. Sweet's office and get down on my knees. Then maybe he'd give me a raise and a health insurance policy that actually took care of my kids instead of this bullshit they offered us.

Who knew how much I was going to end up shelling out after River's current hospital visit?

Fuck. River looked so little in that hospital bed tonight. He was excited I'd brought him a new video game to play. I tried to find something educational, as usual. Boy, my kids were going to be mad when they got a little older and realized there were games out there that were purely for fun and didn't try to teach you anything. *Hey, you can't blame me for trying.*

The breeze coming off the water blew the dress I was wearing around my knees. I felt weird, almost naked, showing up at Marcus's door with my legs bare. He'd never seen them. And I'd worn my hair down. He was probably going to freak when he found out I had rather mousy, nondescript brown hair and not the lovely long, curly raven locks of my Red Velvet Queen wig.

I took a deep breath and depressed the doorbell outside condo #4. Each building had four units, and his was on the far right next to the golf course's hole #9. I'd spent a little longer at the hospital than I'd planned, and now it was 7:30. *Oops.* I promised my mom I'd be home by nine. It didn't look like that was going to happen unless we made this date super fast.

"Jolie!" Marcus exclaimed as he swung the door open. He just stood there for a moment, his mouth hanging open as he took in the image of my real, true self.

I waited for him to say something, anything. He looked only slightly different: no pink polo shirt but a black t-shirt instead. It had a V-neck and was fitted around his biceps just like his work uniform. His hair was the same. Same glasses. Yeah, he was pretty much the same outside of Sweetopia.

"Wow," he stammered, and I couldn't tell if it was a good wow or a bad wow.

I was afraid it was a bad wow. I was too different. I wasn't his fantasy any longer. I'd ruined it.

But before I could dwell any further on my abject failure,

he swept me into his arms, threading his fingers through my real hair as he drew me into his embrace. His lips crashed into mine, leaving me breathless and my mind hopelessly blank.

He pulled back, his hands on my shoulders as his gaze bounced between my eyes. "Jolie...I don't know what to say..."

"Me either." Truer words had never been spoken.

"You look different, but even more beautiful than I could have imagined. I like it." His lips cracked into a smile. "No, I love it."

The way his eyes continued to wander down my bare arms to the smocked bodice of my sundress and then down to my hips where the fabric billowed out in the evening breeze coming off the water sent tingles up and down my spine. I looked around his condo as he shut the door. How did he afford this place? It was nice, with a spacious, open-concept living room and kitchen, and a hallway to the side that must have contained the other rooms.

"Are we going somewhere?" I squeaked out, feeling nearly naked under his intense stare.

But it was different than I expected. Not judgmental. It was a stare of appreciation. Adoration. I never expected him to look at me with even more desire than he did when I was in costume, but here he was proving me oh so very wrong.

His fingertips grazed my bare shoulder, the touch burning through me like his fingers were made of flames. I shuddered, and to my surprise, it elicited the softest, deepest moan, rumbling up his throat like distant thunder.

"I have to be honest with you, Jolie..." His words trailed off as he locked his eyes on mine. "I don't want to go anywhere..."

"You don't?"

He bit his lower lip as he shook his head. "No. I mean, I'm

starving, but all I can think about eating is you. Every. Last. Delicious. Inch." Between each word he planted a kiss along my neck and chest till my knees began to give way, and I fell back into his embrace.

How could he make me this crazy? How could he shift all my stress, all my pain into the deepest corners of my mind and bring my body to the forefront? How could he make every nerve stake its claim over me, all under his unwavering gaze and passionate touch?

"I'd be okay with that." Eating actual food was the furthest thing from my thoughts at the moment. "I can't stay that long, though…"

He didn't question the time limit I was trying to impose. He only reached up to slide the thin strap of my sundress down my arm. "Your skin is so smooth…so beautiful. I really want to see the rest of you."

I held my breath and gave a little nod. Permission acquired, he lifted the dress up over my head. I was wearing a strapless bra underneath, and his gaze immediately fell to my ample breasts rising and falling in their lacy confines. I hoped his attention would stay there instead of lingering on my stretch marks and the slightly sagging skin around my middle. Not to mention my wide hips and thick thighs, which were so expertly concealed in the ballgown I wore as The Red Velvet Queen.

"Breathtaking," was all he said as he moved in a circle around me, pressing soft kisses to my shoulders and moving my hair out of the way to brush a kiss against the back of my neck. I shivered as he made his way around until he was standing in front of me. There was something so reverent in his gaze, worshipful. I couldn't believe the real me seemed to be meeting his expectations. Maybe exceeding them.

I might as well let my true self out. I was no wallflower. I was a Domme, for fuck's sake. Not some shy, demure virgin.

If I was going to show him my true self, I should show him all of it. Nothing held back.

"Have you ever been with an older woman before?" I asked, my courage ramping up.

What's the worst that could happen? That was usually a dangerous question to pose, and I had suffered the curse of that naïve nod to optimism more than once, but, in this case, it was clear he was drinking me in, loving everything his gaze, fingers, and mouth stumbled upon.

"No. Never." He glanced up to see my reaction. "Clearly an oversight on my part…but maybe I was waiting for you."

Between being a Domme and The Fucking Red Velvet Queen, I was going to own all of this. I was a curvy force to be reckoned with, and I vowed to stop worrying about the women Marcus had been with who were his own age. Fuck that. I wasn't getting any younger. And I sure as hell wasn't getting skinny…

"So you like what you see?" My eyes rested against his expectantly.

"Like?" He shook his head. "No, I fucking love it." He took my hand and twirled me around. "You are a masterpiece, Jolie. Who needs to study sculpture in Greece when you have a true goddess standing right before you in the flesh?"

"Greece?" I eyed him curiously.

He laughed and waved his hand to brush off my concern. "I'm going to Greece next week…"

"You are?" I squinted at him. I thought he was a poor college graduate trying to get a real job and make a living. I was just starting to really like him, and he was already leaving the country? That seemed about par for the course.

"Yeah…it's…uh…graduation present from my parents," he explained.

"So you're coming back?"

"Of course I'm coming back." He laughed again. "Why wouldn't I?"

"Well, you're not American. And you're a seasonal worker."

"Right. Well, I'm going to finish out the summer at least." He smiled to reassure me. "Come on now. Do you really want to talk about work?"

CY

I finally had her right where I wanted her, and she was going to grill me about work? *What the fuck?* I clearly needed to turn up the charm. Though I should have been taking the opportunity to glean some useful intel for my parents, I couldn't deny that I was about zero percent interested in my undercover boss gig at the moment and one hundred percent interested in giving this gorgeous creature multiple orgasms.

"No, I don't want to talk about work," she confirmed. Her lips set into a thin line as her stare heated up in intensity. "What I want to do is strip you down and see what you look like under all those clothes."

Now we're talking! "Well, no one's stopping you…"

She bit her lip as she stepped toward me, a seductive swing in her hips, which I could fully appreciate now that she didn't have seven hundred layers of fabric covering them. She grabbed the hem of my black t-shirt and lifted it up. I shrugged out of it and left the whole thing in her hand in the span of about two heartbeats. She seemed impressed by how quickly I made that happen. Then her fingers went to work on my pants, which she deftly unbuttoned and unzipped before sliding them down my thighs.

I stepped out of them, and there I stood before her in all my glory, nothing but a tight pair of black boxer briefs hugging my swelling erection close to my body. All I wanted to do was unleash that beast and have my way with her, but we were finally alone, *really* alone, and we could take our time. Savor each other.

Savor each other? Where the hell did that come from? Cy Sweet was not a savoring type of lover. He was a get in and get off type of guy. Sure, I liked making my partner come too, but not if it took forever. There was definitely a statute of limitations on orgasms.

But Marcus Young had an entirely different M.O.

All Marcus wanted to do was make this beautiful goddess come over and over again, on my tongue, with my fingers, around my cock. And though I wanted to feel bad about being Marcus tonight and not introducing Jolie to Cy, I knew she probably wouldn't like Cy nearly as much.

Hell, even I was starting to prefer Marcus over Cy.

"Goddamn," she breathed out as she stared at my cock, her breasts heaving in her lacy black strapless bra. Her gaze unwavering, she pointed to the bed. "Go lie down."

My eyes jerked to hers. "What?" *She* was giving *me* instructions? *Oh, hell no.*

A devious smile twisted the corners of her lips up. "Yes. Go lie down if you want your cock sucked."

I reached for her hand, which she willingly gave to me. A split second later, I jerked her forward to stand in front of me, and with two hands on her shoulders, I pushed her down until her knees hit the carpet. She grunted in surprise, but when she looked up at me, fire was sparking in her amethyst eyes.

"I'm giving the orders here," I assured her as I lowered my boxer briefs down my thighs, allowing my monstrous cock to spring out into her face.

Her tongue darted out, but I jerked her head back, fisting her shoulder-length brown hair in my hand. She was clearly not accustomed to following orders. Her nostrils flared, and she slightly winced when I tightened my grip.

"Do you want to suck my cock, Jolie?" I forced her to lift her eyes to me with a finger under her chin.

"Yes." She blinked twice, lust swirling in her irises.

"Open your mouth." I waited for her to heed my command, and when she did, I eased the tip between her plump pink lips. I was used to seeing her face painted with thick layers of makeup, but I preferred her like this, a slight flush on her cheeks and just a hint of mascara bringing out her thick lashes. I liked the natural look on her. It was hotter, more primal.

I could tell by the way her eyes watered that she wasn't used to taking a cock as big as mine down her throat. I was as gentle as I could be, but damn if those sweet, juicy lips and tongue working my aching shaft didn't make me want to ram it down fast and hard.

Maybe she had a praise kink? "That's it, Jolie, you are a magnificent cocksucker."

"Mmmmmm," came garbled out of her mouth as she closed her eyes and concentrated on making long, deep strokes up and down my throbbing manhood. Seeing her like that, so raw and vulnerable, only made me want to return the favor. I reached down to hook my hands under her armpits and pulled her off my cock, lifting her until her feet hit the floor.

"What are you doing?" she rasped, her eyes popping open in confusion.

I heaved her over my shoulder and carried her to my bedroom, plopping her down on my king-sized mattress. "I want to taste you too."

Her eyes fluttered half-closed, and she sucked in a sharp

breath as if the sound of my words oozing out had struck her right in the clit. I pulled her on top of me, digging my fingers into the fleshy globes of her voluptuous ass as I positioned her pussy right over my mouth.

She wasted no time wrapping her lips around my cock again, taking it even deeper than she had on her knees. I could barely breathe as she ground her hips into my face, taking what she needed from my lips and tongue while soft moans escaped around my shaft.

I was able to get just enough air in my lungs to instruct her, "Come all over my face, my queen."

Her fingers grasped my thighs as she took me even deeper, enough that she gagged on me as she continued to fuck my face. I couldn't believe how ridiculously hot her writhing against me was, her gorgeous curves undulating as her pussy began to gush hot, sweet juices into my hungry mouth.

Not once did she break suction on my cock, and I swore I wasn't going to come. But as soon as I felt her walls squeezing the two fingers I'd shoved up her tight channel, I completely lost my resolve. My seed rocketed up my shaft and exploded out the head of my cock just as she tightened her lips around it. As my balls drained every last drop they held down her throat, she sucked me dry.

Our bodies both wound down, our orgasms gradually fading along with our moans and racing hearts. I moved out from underneath her, pulling her to rest in the crook of my arm as my other hand stroked down the hourglass curve between her breasts and ass.

I couldn't believe how beautiful she was lying here in my arms. Usually after I came, I had to force myself to stick around, to cuddle with my partner. But in this moment, something deep inside of me was begging to never let her go.

"That was—" she finally attempted to speak.

"—just the beginning," I finished her sentence, guiding her hand between my legs where my cock was beginning to swell again at the idea of filling her sweet pussy.

"I can't stay much longer," she sighed, her voice tapering off to a whisper as the words spilled out.

I didn't answer her, instead flipping her onto her back and sliding between her thighs, which parted to accept me. She didn't really want to leave. That much was abundantly clear. I reached for a condom from the drawer in my nightstand, and she watched me roll it down my shaft with a hungry look in her eyes.

As she lay there, wild and wanton, I thought about the threats my parents made the night before. They wanted me to pump her for information. The only thing I wanted to pump her for was as many orgasms as I could deliver.

There was no way I was ruining tonight with any talk of Sweetopia. Not a chance in hell. I was finally getting to savor the spicy side of The Red Velvet Queen, and I was not about to fuck that up.

The only thing I would be fucking tonight was Jolie. Maybe I'd feel differently in the morning, but for right now, I was living in the moment.

twelve

JOLIE

The next morning, I didn't have the panicked, *jolt awake in bed when my alarm goes off* kind of morning. Instead, the sun wiggled its way past the blinds and gently coaxed my eyes open. I looked around, my consciousness slowly grasping the fact that it was Saturday, and I didn't have to go to work.

That was another thing I had to fight with the Sweets about: weekends off. I negotiated two weekends off a month in the summer. During the school year, the park was closed on Mondays and Tuesdays, so those were my weekends. It wasn't ideal, but it was better than them expecting me to be there every damn day. It was like they thought they'd hired a robot instead of a real, live human being.

I balked at my evil overlord bosses being my first thought of the day. Shaking that nastiness off, I let thoughts of Marcus and our date the night before crash over me like a tidal wave, sweeping away all the negative thoughts. *Oh, yes, that is much better.* I saw flashes of his hands pressed into my skin, his mouth grazing my nipples, and a deep, satisfying soreness reminded me of his massive cock driving into me on repeat.

It was completely breathtaking.

Last night, it took all my strength to fight the urge to collapse in his arms after our romp and drift off to sleep in his warm, safe embrace. My mom said she would stay with River last night, but guilt prevented me from letting her do that. So, when I left Marcus's, I returned to the hospital, where I stayed with River until after midnight before returning home to my bed. I would go back and see my little man later today. I needed to spend some time with Reed first.

I was always dividing myself. Cutting myself into slices like a pie.

I wondered how many slices I had left to give away. Especially after I left a piece of me at Marcus's place last night.

My phone buzzed on my nightstand, and an adrenaline rush raced through me. Through bleary morning vision, I entered my passcode and pulled up the text message, which immediately made me smile.

> Marcus: Wish you were waking up next to me.

I didn't send it, but my first thought was *Oh, I do too, my sexy man.*

There was no way I could explain how badly I wished I were waking up next to him, but that would have meant shirking my responsibilities as a mom. And I couldn't do that. I didn't know how to tell him my son had cystic fibrosis. Not to mention the small fact of my second job. What would he think if he knew I beat old men's asses for money?

Before I could reply, he sent another text.

> Marcus: What are you doing today?

I couldn't exactly tell him the truth. Not over text. Hanging out with Reed. Going to the hospital to see River. Session tonight with a new client. I was going to be busy from the moment I crawled out of bed until the sun set.

> Me: Oh, you know, Mom stuff.

> Marcus: Any time for me? Even just coffee or a drink? I feel bad that I didn't actually take you out last night.

> Me: I'll have to check with my mom. For sitting, you know.

> Marcus: Okay, I'll wait. :)

I headed into the kitchen, where I could hear my mom already rumbling around. If there was indeed a Higher Power looking out for me, my mom would be making coffee. Reed was probably still asleep. It had been way too quiet around our apartment this week with River in the hospital. I couldn't wait to have my little man back home. It wouldn't be much longer now. Dr. Grimes said he was pleased with River's bloodwork since they started the antibiotics.

Maybe things in my life were finally starting to look up? I was seeing an amazing guy. My son seemed to be regaining his health. And the Sweets might actually be forced to get their fucking act together after our meeting Monday night.

"Hey! How was your date with Marcus?" my mom cooed from the corner of the kitchen where she was pouring coffee into a mug. I noticed she had another mug right next to hers, presumably for me. *Best. Mom. Ever.*

I couldn't even answer her question. A long, wistful sigh came out in lieu of a response.

"That good, huh?" She grinned. "I want to hear all about it!"

I let out a raspy chuckle. "Uh, no, I don't think you want those kinds of details." I took the mug she was offering with a grateful smile then fixed it up with cream and sugar.

She smiled and shook her head at me. "When are you seeing him again?"

"He wants to see me today," I answered between sips. "But I'm too busy, really."

"Why not go out tonight? After the boys are asleep? I don't mind." She winked at me. *What is the relationship version of a drug pusher? That's what she is.*

I shook my head as I took yet another sip of coffee, my hands cradling the mug as if it were the Holy Grail. The caffeine was filtering into my bloodstream; I could feel it. "I can't ask you to do that."

"No, I'm telling you. Again." She set down her mug and gave me her "business" look. She'd be breaking out the Italian next if I didn't agree.

"Fine." I rolled my eyes. "I will meet him for like an hour later tonight after my session with the new client."

"That's my girl." Satisfied, she put her empty mug in the sink and went off to gather up laundry.

I grabbed my phone and asked Marcus if we could meet at eight for drinks. It only took him a few seconds to text back a confirmation and address.

I MANAGED TO MAKE IT ON TIME FOR ONCE. IT WAS AMAZING how motivating seeing Marcus was in helping me cross off all the items on my to-do list. Even the session with the new client didn't completely zap me of energy like it normally would. I parked and found Marcus waiting for me right outside the cute little restaurant and bar on a canal in one of the ritzy shopping areas near downtown.

"You look gorgeous." He pressed a kiss to my cheek with a smile that made me go weak in the knees. I almost regretted agreeing to meet him in public instead of having a repeat performance of our romp the night before at his condo. But I was looking forward to getting to know him better. I'd been constantly surprised at how many layers this man seemed to have.

"Thank you." I took his hand as he led me inside. He asked for a booth, a request I doubted they'd be able to grant on a busy Saturday night, but the hostess took one look at Marcus and grinned before immediately ushering us to a booth far in the back of the restaurant, right by the water.

"Wow, that was impressive!" I noted as we sat down.

He cracked open the menu the server had left and winked. "I think my accent gets me special treatment sometimes."

I didn't know if it was his accent or his sexy nerd looks, but either way, it was fun to be out on the town with someone like Marcus. He had this swagger about him, like he owned the world. It was hard to believe he was a recent college grad with a temp gig at Sweetopia. I could hardly imagine what kind of confidence he'd have when he finally secured his dream job. I imagined cashier in The Bard's Bakery was not it.

"What a beautiful night!" I looked out across the canal. The railing was looped with tiny twinkling fairy lights, and all the other lights along the water seemed to be winking back. Live music played across the way from a different restaurant's deck, and the soothing strains floated gently on the warm night breeze. It was just loud enough that it could be enjoyed, but not too loud to inhibit conversation.

"Thank you for agreeing to see me again." Marcus's gaze

rose above the menu and lingered on my face for a moment before drifting down to my cleavage and back up again. "I know you're busy with mom stuff."

I mustered a soft giggle. "Yeah, my two boys keep me busy, that's for sure." I knew this was the perfect time to interject the part about River's condition, but it was such a downer. I didn't want to put any kind of damper on this beautiful evening. There would be plenty of time to tell Marcus when I got to know him better.

Listen to me—talking as if we're an item, a couple.

I was adamantly opposed to it when I first met him, but that was back when I thought he was like most other twenty-something men I'd known: self-absorbed and immature. But Marcus seemed wise beyond his years, and he truly seemed to care about me.

"What are they into? Reed and River, right?" he asked. "Reed is the older one?"

"Wow, good memory!" I was impressed. We'd briefly discussed them the night before, but the main focus of our previous date was our heart-stopping, passionate tango between the sheets. I took a sip of the water the server had brought before answering his question. "They love playing outside, of course. Reed plays soccer and is pretty athletic. River loves books and video games. He's a bit of a nerd like his mom."

"Hey, nerds rule," Marcus interjected with a wide smile. "Proud nerd here!"

"I love that about you," I admitted. "I've always had a bit of a thing for nerds…"

"Lucky me!" He flagged down the waitress and proceeded to order us two alcoholic drinks.

I felt like such an adult all the sudden, which was weird because I always got to experience the non-fun parts of adulting: taking care of kids, working two jobs and paying bills. But I rarely got to partake of the fun parts: indulging in adult drinks, staying out late, or enjoying sex. This week, it was like all the fun adult stuff I'd missed out on during the past few years was being crammed into two nights.

Maybe it was just the start of a new and exciting adult adventure for me? I was almost too scared to hope for it.

"So, I'm guessing Sweetopia is just a stepping stone to what you really want to do with your life. Right?" I asked while we waited for our drinks to arrive.

"You could say that," he answered, his eyes flickering with passion. "I'm actually somewhat of an artist. I've been studying art since I was your son's age, and I've gotten to do a fair amount of traveling to check out ancient and Renaissance pieces. I'm really into both time periods. That's why I'm going to Greece here soon—to study sculpture with Kristoph Kostopoulos, the famous art historian and archaeologist."

"And Sweetopia is going to let you leave during the middle of the busy season like that?" It did seem strange that I could barely get a weekend off, but the Sweets would let some summer temp come and go as he pleased. They didn't have a backup Red Velvet Queen though. If I wasn't there, there was no meet and greet in the throne room, only the one with the Donut Dragon in the Dragon's Lair.

"Oh, well, yeah, it was arranged way in advance," he explained. "Like I said, the accent helps a lot." He winked again, probably his third wink of the evening.

Is winking a British thing? I wondered.

"What do you plan to do with all your art knowledge?" I pressed a little harder. "Do you plan to pursue a career in art?"

"Good question." The server arrived right then with our drinks, which were a pretty coral color. He took a sip of his and swirled the liquid and ice around in its glass for a moment. "I honestly don't know yet. I guess I will have to go back to school at some point. MFA maybe? Maybe teaching? Or work at a museum?"

It seemed a little strange to me that he didn't have a little better idea what he wanted to do, but who was I to talk? I dropped out of college and wanted to pursue an acting career for what seemed like forever, and what had I achieved? I was a costumed character at a children's theme park and a dominatrix. And I was six years older than Marcus. I was not one to judge when it came to setting and achieving career goals.

"What about you?" His eyes lifted from the drink to meet mine. And there was that smoldering look again, the one that said he wanted to rip my clothes off and have his way with me. I really liked that look.

"Well, right now I just want to make it through the week," I said with a sardonic laugh. It wasn't untrue, even if it did sound pathetic. "But eventually I want to be an actress. I was hoping this Red Velvet Queen gig would lead to something with Sweet Enterprises, but I don't think they like me much."

"No?" He raised his eyebrows. "Why not?"

I shrugged then followed it up with an eye roll, because of course I knew the reason. "They really want a robot, but they got a real person instead. You know, one with a need for breaks and days off and fair compensation. That sort of thing."

He continued to stare into my eyes, but his expression didn't waver. I wasn't sure what that meant. That he thought I was exaggerating? That he thought I had a persecution complex?

That he was on the Sweets' side? How could anyone be on their side?

CY

Maybe she was more involved in this employee uprising than I previously believed. *But she's so busy with her kids—and she's relatively new at the park—she can't be the one organizing it.*

It was probably Colleen. Colleen was the name I should give up to my parents. She and Buster were likely behind it. I didn't want to say anything that might get Jolie in trouble—she needed this job. Maybe I could put in a good word so she could get The Red Velvet Queen role on the silver screen—*if there is a movie...*

"Marcus?" came her soft voice floating across the table.

I didn't know where my mind had wandered off to, but she had already finished half her cocktail. "Sorry, I spaced out there for a moment. Do you want another? Something to eat?"

She giggled. Maybe the alcohol was affecting her already. "No, nothing to eat. Another one of these might be nice. So fruity!"

"Yep, my man Carlos behind the bar just added this to their summer menu. Fresh mango. Can't go wrong with fresh mango."

She just stared at me like *how the hell are you on a first-name basis with Carlos?*

"I used to work here," I lied. *Duh, that was stupid.* Especially after I said I got a table because of my accent.

The truth was that I came there a lot with Clem, and with Carson too, if he could ditch the ball-and-chain for the evening. Going out drinking with my bros was one of the only things the three of us did together.

Confusion flickered across her features, but she took a long sip of the cocktail to finish it off. *Good.* Maybe she wouldn't realize what I said before about my accent getting me special treatment, or she'd think I was joking about it.

God, I feel like such a tool. Would she even like me if she knew who I really was? Or maybe she would like me more if she knew I had money? She didn't seem like the gold-digger type, though.

I was eager to change the subject. "So how much time do you have tonight?"

She glanced down at her phone, which she'd placed on the table next to her pocketbook. She was always on alert. I wished I could help her relax. Take her out of constant vigilance mode for a day or two. "Maybe an hour? Sorry I can't stay longer."

I wondered how many times I would get to see her before I left for Greece next week. I needed to make the most of every moment. I hated to say this, but I was going to miss her when I was gone. I wished I could ask her to come with me. I knew it could never happen, what with her job and her kids, but I would be lying if I denied fantasizing about it a time or two.

I bet I could get her to relax in Santorini...

"Maybe we can walk along the canal for a bit after our second round?" I searched her face for clues she was beginning to have feelings for me as well.

Feelings? I don't do feelings.

I couldn't even sleep last night, I was so high on the endorphins that flooded my body when I fucked her senseless. Only that second round, it didn't feel like fucking. It felt like something different...something more intense, more meaningful.

What we did last night...was it making love?

She laid her hand on top of mine and locked her amethyst eyes with my deep, dark browns. "I really like you, Marcus."

"Good, I really like you too," I fired back more confidently than I was feeling.

"You're just so real. So down to earth. I really appreciate that. I can't handle fake people. Ain't nobody got time for that, right?" She smiled, then the server stopped by, interrupting the moment.

I ordered two more drinks as her words sank in. *She thinks I'm real. Down to earth.*

Fuck.

Marcus is real. Down to earth.

Cy is a real spoiled brat.

Maybe I wasn't really Cy anymore? I needed to come clean before I left for Greece. If she could forgive me, maybe we could pursue something…more serious…when I returned?

There had to be a way to give my parents what they wanted, keep my inheritance, and get the girl too.

I was smart. I could figure this out.

After we finished our second round of drinks, I paid the tab, and we left, hand in hand, to stroll along the moonlit canal. The silver moonbeams dappled on the water, streaked with the reflection of all the golden lamps dotting the sidewalks on each side. Jolie's hand felt so small and soft in mine. I knew she was six years older than me, but something about her was so delicate and vulnerable. I wanted to take care of her, wanted to protect her.

I couldn't remember ever feeling that way before about anyone.

The canal crossed over the street and curved its way toward the beach. I loved all the water in my hometown. Getting to walk on the beach with this beautiful creature would be the highlight of my night. Amidst the croaking frogs and crickets' serenade, we stepped off the sidewalk onto the cool silver sand. Twenty yards ahead, the gulf gently lapped at the shore.

"Want to walk along the water?" I squeezed her hand in mine.

"Yes, but I need to leave pretty soon…" She sighed then reached down to take off her sandals, letting her bare feet sink into the sand. I followed suit, and then we made our way across the beach toward the water.

"Oh, it's so warm!" She giggled as the waves rushed over her feet. I wished I could bottle up that sound, this moment so I could play it back someday when I was feeling lost or sad. No matter how thick the clouds overhead were, this memory could clear them all and bring out the sun. I was sure of it.

I couldn't bear to go another moment without my lips on hers, so I wrapped my arms around her, pulling her toward me. I would stand here with the waves rolling over our feet, the scent of the sea perfuming the night, devouring her for as long as she would let me.

thirteen

"Well, someone seems to be in a good mood this morning!" Mom called down the hall. "Did you have fun last night?

"I did," I fully admitted as I set the laundry basket down on the kitchen table. "Gosh, it's really nice to go out and enjoy adult beverages and conversation."

"So, are you serious about this guy?" She blinked a couple of times as she searched my face for the answers I wouldn't verbalize.

"I don't know about serious," I answered—not a lie. "He's younger than me and doesn't know much about my situation with the boys. I don't know how much interest he has in a commitment to a woman with kids, you know? It's too soon, anyway. I just want to have fun."

I did just want to have fun, but when I thought about Marcus going to Greece… Maybe I wouldn't see him again? Maybe he wouldn't return to Sweetopia? That thought stabbed my gut and caused a deep ache.

My mom stepped closer to me, pulled me into her arms and pressed a kiss to my cheek. "I'm glad you realize you deserve to have fun," she said. "You've punished yourself long enough for what happened with the boys' fathers. And for River being sick. None of that is your fault. And you've been the absolute best mother you can be for those boys."

"I still have my doubts." I shook my head. "Still feel like I could do more, be better for them. But I deserve some me-time too."

"That's my girl. How's the stuff with Sweetopia going?"

I shrugged. "We'll find out soon. I think the plan is coming together nicely."

She smiled. "Fingers crossed. All your hard work is going to pay off."

CY

I'd be lying if I didn't admit there was a little extra spring in my step as I bounced into the castle that Monday morning in my pink Sweetopia polo shirt. Though I would have loved for Jolie to spend the night after our epic romp on Friday night or our moonlit stroll on the beach on Saturday, I did understand she had to take care of her sons. I left her to that all of yesterday, but I couldn't get her off my mind. I still couldn't believe I was dating a MILF.

Me, *dating*? I didn't know if that was really what to call it, but we had definitely progressed past hooking up in her dressing room. That wasn't going to stop me from heading to see her there before work, though. I just couldn't seem to get enough of her.

I took a right, then a left, aiming toward the bakery, when

I was suddenly tackled from behind. "What the fuck?!" I glanced behind me to find my older brother Clem hanging on my back. "Get the fuck off me, dude!"

"Hey, were you whistling?" When he jumped off me, I noticed his company polo shirt was a light gray color. That seemed patently unfair.

"Whistling? Do I look like the type of guy who whistles?" I was so used to having my accent in this building that it came out automatically.

"What, you're pretending to be British now?" He pursed his lips as he looked me up and down. "And since when do you wear glasses?"

"It's part of the disguise, dumbass. Remember? Under-cover boss?" I whispered the last part. Still kept the accent up, though.

"Knock off the accent, for fuck's sake. You sound ridicu-lous." He rolled his eyes.

"Too late now. Everyone here knows I have it!" I beamed at him.

"Including The Red Velvet Queen, right? I know you're banging her." He shoved me at the shoulder, knocking me back against the concrete wall of the tunnel.

"What the hell was that for? And how is it any of your business who I bang?" I seethed. Then I thought of Jolie, and my scowl faded. "By the way, I prefer the term 'make sweet love to.' Get it?"

"As long as you're pumping her for information, it's my business. You know, some people think she's the mastermind behind all the negative press we're getting." Clem folded his arms across his chest. "I can't say I blame you, though. She is the perfect target. Hot as hell too."

I glared at him. Even though I'd heard him and Carson talking about her before, now that I'd gotten to know her—especially intimately—I found their comments completely obnoxious and unwarranted. She was mine now, and I wouldn't stand for them ogling her like a prime piece of meat.

"So, the queen *does* put out, then? Is she any good?" Clem continued, and I had to fight off the urge to pop him in the mouth. "Even more importantly, have you gotten her to call off the strike? Or the press conference tomorrow night?"

"Marcus?" came a familiar voice behind me.

Fuck. It was Colleen.

I shot my brother a glare but didn't say a word. He waved to Colleen and then disappeared in the direction she had come from.

She cocked her head to stare at me. "You know Clem Sweet?"

"A little," I answered with no hesitation. "He hired me… and my sister used to date him."

Where were these lies coming from? They were flying off my tongue like arrows shot from a bow. Arrows I had absolutely no control over.

"I see." Her eyes never left mine as she crossed her arms in front of her. I could tell from those two little words that her suspicions had not been quelled.

"So, the location for the meeting tonight?" I reminded her.

Her brows furrowed for a second, and then a small smile curled her lips. "It's been rescheduled."

"Really?" I wanted to mention the media thing happening tomorrow, the press conference Clem just mentioned, but then I'd have to explain how I knew that.

She shrugged. "It's not up to me."

"So do I get an invite?" I pressed.

She shrugged again. "Also not up to me. We'll see." She brushed past me and headed toward the bakery. "Why are you late, anyway?"

She was clearly just as late as I was.

Footsteps pounded down the long, cavernous hallway, bouncing off the concrete block walls. Jolie appeared, chest heaving as she gasped for air.

"Guess we're all running late this morning!" Colleen observed and rolled her eyes. She glanced over her shoulder at Jolie and looked for a moment like she was about to say something, but then thought better of it.

"Are you okay?" I whispered to Jolie, and she nodded, not saying a word but throwing her gaze toward Colleen as if to tell me she didn't want my boss to overhear our conversation.

"I'll come visit at lunch," I whispered back, and she nodded before darting down the hallway opposite the bakery, which led to the throne room.

JOLIE

I'd never been so eager for lunch as I was today. I almost drop-kicked the last kid in line over to her parents and yelled, "See ya, wouldn't want to be ya!" at the top of my lungs right before the ropes fell, announcing my break. *Not exactly queen-like, huh?*

This weekend with Marcus—though we only had about four hours together total—was undoubtedly the most amazing weekend I'd ever had with a man. Friday's date was the best sexual experience I'd ever had in my life—hands down. I a) couldn't believe he was so young with as much poise and control as he had in bed, and b) couldn't believe how many orgasms he gave me. Furthermore, I was astounded by how much I enjoyed him taking control. Just thinking about it was making my womanly bits tingle with desire.

When I got back to my dressing room at 12:05, he was waiting for me right outside the door with the most adorable little knowing smile on his face. He waited for me to get the door shut behind him before he pressed a kiss against my lips. Then he went right for my neck, but I had to cut him off there.

"You can't be starting that," I warned him, "or neither of us will ever get back to work. And now that I've had the full monty, so to speak, I don't think I'll ever be satisfied with dressing room quickies again."

His lips spread into a devious grin. "Is that so? Well, I was going to say I didn't think you could stroke my ego any more after the other night, but I was clearly mistaken."

He's so fuckin' cute!

I just wanted to kiss that salacious smile right off his face, strip that pink polo over his head, and sink my teeth into him. One of the things that kept going through my mind about last weekend was how dominant he was. Not in a cruel way, not like I was with my clients—how they wanted me and paid me to be.

Marcus was dominant in a demanding, greedy way. Like he just couldn't get enough of me. I never thought I would enjoy that so much, but fuck. It was hot as hell.

"Are you going to eat your lunch?" He made himself comfortable in the wingback chair in the corner. I sank onto my stool at my vanity, my skirts gathering around me as I reached down into my mini fridge to pull out my lunch bag.

"I made one for you too." I tossed him a sandwich. "Hope you like chicken salad."

"Wow, it's on a croissant. Fancy!" He laughed as he caught the plastic bag in his hand.

"One advantage of dating a mom—we always bring snacks." I smiled as I watched him unwrap the sandwich.

He chuckled at that, but he needed to know—being a mom was a huge part of my identity. If we were going to have any sort of relationship, he needed to know my sons came first.

But…I wasn't ready to reveal everything just yet.

I'd picked up the sandwiches in the hospital cafeteria this morning on my way out after stopping to relieve my mom and see River, but I couldn't tell Marcus that. There was a lot he didn't know about me yet, but I wanted to come clean —soon.

After Saturday night, I realized that someone as open, honest, and transparent as he was about his situation deserved the same from me. In some ways, it seemed like we were both struggling. He was trying to make it abroad, create a life for himself here and avoid having to go back to England. He was torn between his passion for art and his need to support himself. I knew exactly how that felt. We were cut from the same cloth.

"Is the chicken salad that good, or do I have it all over my face?" he asked, drawing me out of my thoughts.

"It's pretty good. Why?"

"You just have such a beautiful smile on your face," he observed. "It's contagious, I think."

His accent colored all of his words with so much spark and sunlight that I couldn't help but beam. "Sorry, you just have that effect on me. It had been forever since I'd gone on a…date…if that's what we're calling what happened this weekend?"

"I think it's safe to call it that." He took another bite and chewed as if he'd just bitten off a piece of victory.

"I feel like I got to know you more in those four hours

than in the, what has it been, three weeks now that we've known each other?"

"Ah, pillow talk with actual pillows will do that," he agreed. "I only wish we'd ended our date Saturday night the same way. I feel like I've known you much longer."

I nodded. It did feel that way. We had such a strong connection.

He told me Saturday how he had grown up the son of a single mom, how he and his siblings never really knew their dad. He was the youngest in his family and the first to go to university and to America. It made me think that maybe Reed and River had a shot at a normal life, of achieving more than I could have ever dreamed of.

His smile faded a bit as his eyes trailed across my face. "You didn't share as much about you, though. You let me do most of the talking during our Saturday session."

I wasn't accustomed to hearing the word "session" used like that. I used that term to describe my appointments with my clients. "Sessions" and "appointments." That was the vocabulary I felt most comfortable with—business transaction terms. It seemed appropriate for that line of work. It didn't seem right for what Marcus and I shared this weekend.

How could I tell him I moonlighted as a dominatrix? I was afraid once he found out about my other job, he wouldn't want me anymore. *Not to mention how sick River is...*

I sighed. It wasn't going to be easy, but he'd made me feel so accepted, so desired, a small part of me wanted to believe that laying all my cards on the table could only strengthen our connection.

Listen to me! My how things change...

A week ago, I wouldn't have even considered letting him into my inner circle or letting him be privy to the crazy life I was dealt. Him and that magic cock, that magic smile, magic accent…it was just too much for me to fight any longer.

The more I learned about Marcus Young, the more unbelievably right he became. He was a one-in-a-million shot. So special, I was considering telling him about my plans to hold Sweetopia accountable for the way they'd hurt me, hurt my children. The more I spoke with Marcus, the more I saw him as an asset. An ally.

"I'm glad you asked, to be honest. There's a lot I want to share with you. I don't know if we have enough time right now, though." I glanced up at the clock. It was already 12:30. How did twenty-five minutes fly by with us just sitting here nibbling on these sandwiches? It seemed to defy the space/time continuum.

"More than you having two kids?" His eyebrows flew up. "To be honest, that was pretty surprising to me, but I think it's awesome. I know you're a great mom."

I bit my lip, stalling while I tried to figure out what to say. "Well, there's a little more to it than that. And I need to tell you about my second job—"

I stopped talking when I noticed him patting his pants pocket. He held up one finger as he retrieved his phone, pulling it out to glance down and see who was calling. "Oh, shit, it's Colleen. I better take this."

He put the phone to his ear, the smile he had worn seconds ago fading into oblivion. "Okay. Yeah, I can come back. No problem. Just a sec." He frowned, pursing his lips as he returned the phone to his pocket.

"What's wrong?"

He rolled his eyes. "Sorry, Colleen said she needs me to come back to the bakery right away."

"Oh." I stood up as soon as he did, hoping I would at least get a kiss goodbye. In a way, this was good. I could sit on my throne all day on autopilot while I figured out how I wanted to tell him about River's CF and my second job as a Mistress Magenta. Those were the two main things I figured anyone getting into a relationship with me ought to know.

"Sorry. I can drop by after work…" He paused for a moment as if his memory was kicking in. "Oh, is that meeting tonight?"

The meeting had been postponed till tomorrow, but I didn't want to talk to him about that yet. I wanted to see how he reacted to the other stuff first. And then I would tell him about my involvement in the Rebel Alliance, which is what we called our organization that was plotting to take down the Sweets and their Evil Enterprise once and for all. Considering how much Corden Sweet reminded me of Darth Vader (minus the black suit, helmet, and breathing issues), it seemed incredibly apropos.

"I'll text you, okay?" I gave him a sweet smile and reached my arms out to offer him a hug.

He scooped me up into his embrace and planted a kiss on my lips. "I'll see you soon."

fourteen

CY

I breezed through the kitchen, catching sight of Colleen in the cramped glass-walled office in one corner. The time clock was right outside the square enclosure, and that was pretty much the closest I ever got to her office. My boss was never in it because she was always working her ass off out front with the rest of us. Until now. As soon as she saw me, she gestured for me to come inside.

"Hey, sorry, I thought I had a little more time for lunch," I apologized as I took a seat in the hard plastic chair across from her desk. She was reading something on her computer, but when she did finally look at me, I saw a fire in her eyes I'd never seen before. It almost looked like rage.

"Close the door, Marcus," she barked at me.

Whoa. I had never heard her sound like that before. What the fuck had I done?

I reached over to swing the door shut, not realizing how hard I pushed it. It crashed into the frame with a bang, which only seemed to make the scowl on Colleen's face deepen. "What's going on? Is there a problem?"

Her eyes whipped toward me, locking on to mine as her intense glare ramped up. "Yeah, there's a problem." She adjusted her computer monitor, turning it around to a photo on the Sweetopia website.

Of my family.

With me in it.

Oh shit.

"You want to explain to me why you look exactly like the Sweet's youngest son?" There was a nasty sneer in her voice.

I scraped my hand down my beard, which had grown in nice and thick. "Oh, I do look a wee bit like the Sweet chap, don't I?"

She huffed out a breath as she turned the monitor back toward her. "You know, when I saw you chatting with Clem in the hallway earlier this morning, it all became crystal-fucking-clear. You're here undercover, aren't you?"

"What?" I mustered up as much shock and outrage as I could. "I don't know what you're talking about." My fake accent held steady.

"Stop with the fake British accent already," she snapped. "I understand now why you've asked so many questions about the meeting, about the secret Facebook group. Your parents sent you in here as an undercover boss, didn't they? They couldn't send Clem or Carson because we all know who they are, but you've barely worked in the park, right? You've been gallivanting all over the globe studying art."

Fuck.

"Are you the one organizing the employee uprising?" I asked, finally dropping the accent. There was no sense in beating around the bush now.

"No, I'm not, but there is no fucking way in hell I'm giving you any more information about it," she seethed. The veins in her temple looked to be throbbing, and her jaw was clenched so tight, I thought it might snap.

"You know your job is on the line, right?" I reminded her. "All I have to do is say the word, and they'll fire you."

She ignored that little truth nugget and attacked from a different angle. "And that's why you've been getting close to Jolie, isn't it? You're trying to figure out how she's involved in all this, aren't you?"

"No, actually, I really like her." That wasn't a lie, even if it was a little hard for me to admit it to someone else.

Colleen looked me up and down, the wheels clearly turning in her head. "I won't blow your cover, and I won't tell your parents you've been goofing off with one of their employees instead of doing whatever the hell you're supposed to be doing, if—"

"If what?"

How dare she threaten me! I could fire this woman. My parents would back me up on that, right?

Ugh. I didn't know that they would at this point. The last time I talked to my dad, he was pretty disgusted with my performance thus far.

"If you stay away from Jolie," she sneered. "I mean it. No going to her dressing room. No talking to her if she comes in here."

"But I already told you, my mission here has nothing to do with Jolie. I genuinely like her!" I didn't mean to raise my voice, but it was too late. I wondered how soundproof these glass walls were.

"You Sweets are all the same, you know that? You think of people in terms of what they can do for you instead of being actual human beings with needs and feelings. It's sick, really."

Colleen shook her head as she continued to shoot daggers at me. "Jolie deserves better than that. She's a good, kind, young woman and a hell of a mom. I don't want her getting mixed up with you—and if she finds out you're the Sweets' son, she might be tempted—"

"Tempted? Because of my money?" I shook my head. That didn't sound like the Jolie I had gotten to know.

Colleen sighed. "No, she's not a gold digger, if that's what you're afraid of." She flared her nostrils as another deep breath huffed out her mouth. "Look, this isn't my story to tell, but if you care about her, you'll stay away from her. She has enough on her plate. She only needs loyal, reliable, trustworthy people surrounding her, and you're not it."

"Why? She's an adult. She can make her own choices," I protested.

"Her kid is sick, okay?" Colleen fired at me.

It was a flaming arrow that pierced me right in the heart. "What do you mean, sick?" The story Buster told us last week of the park employee with a terminally ill child came to mind.

"Her younger son has cystic fibrosis," she filled me in. "He's been in the hospital getting a high-power course of IV antibiotics for the past few days."

"What?" I shook my head in disbelief as I flashed back to our conversation in her dressing room just moments ago. She said there was more she wanted to tell me, more that I should know.

Here she was about to bare her secrets to me, show me who she really was beneath the crown, the costume. And she still had no fucking clue who I was. She didn't even know my real name.

Maybe Colleen was right. Maybe I didn't deserve her.

"You heard me. Now, look, you need to come up with something to tell your parents, and if you really care about Jolie, you'll protect her. She doesn't need any more shit in her life, and she really needs this job, okay?" Colleen's dark eyes were blazing with compassion. She cared about Jolie a great deal. That much was obvious.

My mind was racing, and my temples were starting to pound as the situation I'd found myself stuck in became clearer and clearer. The expression "between a rock and a hard place" came to mind. I was wedged in there so tight, I could barely breathe.

I heaved a sigh as my elbows went to my knees, propping up my head as my hands scrubbed down my face. "My parents are breathing down my neck. They want details on the meeting and this media shit going down. I don't know what to tell them. I can't make everyone happy here."

And that was the honest truth of the matter. I'd never cared about making anyone happy before, and all of the sudden, I found myself wanting to be on everyone's good side.

"I don't think you're a bad person, Cy," she said, using my real name. "Not if there has been any truth at all behind your portrayal of 'Marcus.' But your parents are two selfish, greedy assholes. And I have a feeling your two older brothers are just as bad. Things at Sweetopia will probably get even worse with them at the helm. That's why the employees are banding together now, getting our ducks in a row. We want to stand up to them, force them to do what's right—"

"But if Sweetopia shuts down, you'll all lose your jobs. What are you calling for…a strike? A boycott?"

Her eyes gleamed, even though she didn't confirm or deny my accusation. "Once the media breaks the story of a single mom who can't get the treatment she needs for her terminally ill son because of the Sweets' ridiculously expensive and useless health plan…"

Oh, god, Jolie *was* the organizer. Or if she wasn't, she was definitely the poster child. Their entire operation hinged on her and her story.

Colleen's dark eyes stabbed into me. "You have a chance to do the right thing, Cy."

Rushing blood roared in my ears as the weight of all these realizations pressed down on me. "If I don't give up the name of the person behind this…this…union you're organizing, then I'm toast. They're cutting me off."

"It's up to you," she reiterated. "You're going to have to make a choice. And you don't have much time."

JOLIE

I had no idea where Marcus was. It was past the time he'd agreed to meet me, and he still hadn't shown up in my dressing room. Maybe I'd scared him off with my warning that I wanted to share some things he needed to know about me. I wasn't supposed to be venturing outside the throne room or my dressing room during work hours, but I could use the employee tunnels to get to the bakery. Hopefully no one would see me. I'd just check if he got held up over there.

Colleen was in her office when I made my way through the storage room and kitchen from the tunnel. I knocked lightly on the glass so I wouldn't scare her, but she jumped anyway.

"Hey," I poked my head in, "have you seen Marcus?"

She tilted her head for a moment as if she had to think about it. Then her brows furrowed as she gestured for me to come in and have a seat.

"What's up?" I arranged my skirt around my legs. It was so voluminous, it barely fit between the chair and the desk where she sat.

She fixed her dark gaze on me. "Have you and Marcus been…uh…dating?"

I wasn't expecting to be interrogated about my private life, but Colleen knew me well enough. She was aware of my situation with River and how I didn't have help from either of my sons' fathers.

I settled on, "Well, we're just…getting to know each other."

"Getting to know each other in a *romantic* way?" she pushed, her eyebrows arching.

I shrugged. "I guess you could say that."

She huffed out a long breath as she continued to stare at me. "I don't know if that's such a good idea, hun."

"Why not?" Was she judging me for not being with my kids every moment I wasn't at work? She didn't know about my dominatrix gig. That was just about the only thing she didn't know about me. Maybe she didn't think I should date, that I should be in Mom Mode any time I wasn't at work.

I guess that's what I thought too—up until a few days ago.

She cleared her throat as she seemed to struggle with how to articulate her thoughts. "I just don't know if Marcus is really who he appears to be," she warned me. "I don't have any concrete evidence, but a couple things aren't adding up."

"Like what?" My heart was beginning to thump hard against my ribs, and the pressure from my corset wasn't helping.

"I can't give you anything just yet. Give me some time," she said. "By the time of the meeting, I should know more."

"Is this why you wanted to change the date and time?" We had been set to meet tonight. She talked me into changing it, and I was actually good with that decision because River was still in the hospital, and I really wanted to be with him tonight.

"Partially," she revealed. "Just…stay away from him, okay, Jolie? You have to trust me on this."

I shook my head as my heart raced. The flood of regret and confusion surging through me was enough to make me sick to my stomach. I just wanted a low-key summer fling. I should have known better than to actually invest any emotion in this guy.

Well, I did know better—at first. I didn't know when things changed, but obviously I'd let my heart take over when I should have kept that bitch chained up.

"Alright. I better get out of here. So Marcus already left for the day?" I scanned outside the glass walls of her office, searching for him in the fluorescent-lighted kitchen just outside. Tall metal shelves with flour, sugar, and other ingredients partially obstructed my view.

"He went to the gift shop to get some ibuprofen," she told me. "He's working late tonight."

He wasn't the only one feeling bad. "Okay. Thanks."

"If I don't see you before, I'll see you tomorrow night at The Roost, okay?"

The Roost was where the secret employee meeting was being held. I needed to confirm with all the media outlets who were planning to cover my story. What no one knew besides Colleen was that it wasn't a meeting to plan the agenda for the press conference. It was the actual press conference itself. It was a prime-time news slot, and it would be followed up with an employee strike at the park the next morning. At the same time, the public would be asked to boycott Sweetopia until the Sweets agreed to our terms.

I was still ironing out the terms with Colleen and a few other park employees who were in our inner circle, but they included raises across the board, flex time for working parents, better and more affordable healthcare coverage, and an actual overtime rate. Nothing we were asking for was unreasonable. We just wanted a living wage and the caliber of benefits we knew the Sweets could afford based on how much the park brought in annually. Oh, we'd done our research. It was more difficult with the park being privately owned, but we had an ally in the accounting office who put together numbers for us.

My mind swirling with how much still needed to be done before the "meeting," I decided to take a cue from Marcus and also sneak into the gift shop for some painkillers. Though Ellie, the gift shop manager, wasn't in the "inner circle," she was definitely sympathetic to our cause and would be in attendance at the meeting. I was sure she'd slip me a few pills if I texted her from the storeroom, the only place I could get while still in costume.

I said goodbye to Colleen and rushed back down the employee tunnel, taking a couple of turns till I arrived at the back door of the gift shop. I thought the door would be locked, but I found it just a little bit ajar, like someone had forgotten to close it the whole way.

"Ellie?" I called out into the dark space, but I didn't hear anything, so I crossed the threshold and proceeded through a short hallway lined with shelves. I wasn't sure where the light switch was, so I kept walking, coming to an abrupt stop when I heard some whispering.

I could tell the whispering was coming from the other side of the shelving unit, and when I rose up on my tiptoes, there was a space to look through to the other side. I had to raise my hand to my lips to stifle the sharp gasp that escaped when I saw Marcus and Ellie standing mere inches from each other.

Ellie had her hand on Marcus's shoulder and reached out to run her fingers through his hair. I thought he'd flinch or back away, but, no, he just stood there. There was a bit more whispering, which I couldn't decipher, then he wrapped his arms around her waist and aligned his lips with hers. Next thing I knew, he was kissing her.

Kissing her! What the actual fuck?

I didn't think I made a noise, but maybe I inadvertently did. He abruptly jerked away from her and said something else I couldn't understand. By that point in time, my heart was pounding so hard, the sound of blood whooshing through my ears was the only thing I could hear.

"See you then," Ellie's nasal voice filled the quiet room. Marcus nodded and turned to leave.

I guess I didn't realize he would be coming back to the doorway where I was still standing. *Duh.*

"Jolie?"

Oh shit!

I turned and fled down the hall, hearing his footsteps trailing me. It was nearly impossible to run in my heels, but I suddenly turned into a track star, hightailing it back to my dressing room like I was aiming for a gold medal at the Olympics.

His footsteps pounded into the concrete floor of the tunnel behind me, but I reached my dressing room door just as he was turning the corner. I slammed it shut, and seconds later, heavy fists began to hammer against it.

I collapsed in the chair in the corner of my dressing room, fighting off the tears threatening to ruin my makeup. I was not going to cry over that asshole. I should have known he was a player.

Colleen must have known about him and Ellie. That was why she was trying to warn me about him. Maybe he said something to her about Ellie, and she'd been reticent to give me her name because of her involvement in the Rebel Alliance.

Fuck. I was glad I caught them, though. Better to find out now before I invested any more of my time and energy in him. I had bigger fish to fry. *That fucking bastard.*

At least I'd managed to avoid having to talk to him.

But I didn't get anything for my splitting headache, which was now ten times worse.

fifteen

CY

Family dinners should never be this awkward. I was sitting across from my brother Carson and his wife, with Clem beside me and my parents at opposite ends of the table. I was waiting for my parents to grill me about what happened at work, but they were obviously going to postpone the grilling until Maureen served the rest of the dishes.

The potatoes came out steaming. The roast looked like perfection with its halo of carrots and asparagus artfully arranged around it, and the aroma from the basket of rolls wafted through the blue and white striped towel wrapped around it. I just wished I had more of an appetite.

As soon as Maureen scurried back to the kitchen, my father's eyes swung in my direction. He didn't even have to say anything, he just stared at me.

Finally, when I didn't respond, my mother added, "Well?"

"Well, what?" I shrugged.

I'd been battling the angel on one shoulder and devil on

the other for the better part of the afternoon. I couldn't decide what to do, but I was fairly confident I was screwed either way.

I could tell my parents about the meeting and who the organizers were, and they could nip it in the bud before it could happen. I had a location and a time, thanks to my little rendezvous with Ellie. I could give up that information and save my inheritance. And, you know, prevent myself from becoming a homeless bum. *Always a plus.*

And collect my $25,000. I mean, that was part of the plan, no?

Or I could tell them to go to hell and let the Sweetopia employees have their little meeting to finalize their list of demands for their strike. It wasn't as if my parents didn't deserve everything they were being served.

I spent part of my afternoon, when I wasn't busy wrestling with the proverbial angel and demon, doing some research in the company books. Colleen basically told me to get lost for the rest of the day; she didn't want to see me. So, I found a computer with wi-fi over in the arcade office. Buster said he didn't mind if I fooled around on it. I concocted some sort of bullshit story for why I needed it, but I was actually hacking into a bunch of tax and banking info.

I might have been an art history junkie in college, but I also happened to be a whiz with computers. Always had been. I didn't see much of a reason to pursue it as a career because, *hello*, silver spoon and all that. So I picked something I was passionate about: art. But I could hack in and do some programming and other technical crap. I didn't think my parents had any idea about the extent of my abilities, or they probably would have put me to work on writing software programs for the park or creating databases or something. *Ugh, that shit is so boring.*

Anyway, everything Colleen, Buster, and Jolie had told

me in the past few weeks was absolutely correct. Actually, it was even worse than they thought because it turned out my parents made a hell of a lot more money than even I imagined. And I'd already known they were filthy stinkin' rich.

Some of the assets were hidden in separate trust funds set up for my brothers and me, and my parents were constantly shifting money in there so they wouldn't have to pay taxes on it. The three of us were their bouncing baby tax shelters.

I was shocked to discover an account with my name on it with over twenty-five mil in it.

TWENTY-FIVE MILLION DOLLARS!

And here they were trying to entice me with a mere 25K. Hell, it was probably coming out of my own account that they'd been building since I was in elementary school. The deposits actually went back that far.

"Cyrus Anthony!" my mother yelled, startling me back to the dinner table where my brothers had both begun to dig into their meals.

My father sat clenching his fork in one hand and steadily sipping on what looked to be scotch with the other. He was looking increasingly stabby the longer I refrained from answering my mother.

"What?!" I thundered back at them.

"What did you find out today?" My mother turned on a dime, making her voice pleasant and light, like we were enjoying a tea-time discussion about tending heirloom roses.

"Did you talk to Ms. Cox?" my father pressed. He shot a look over to my brother Clem, who raised his eyebrows at me in expectation.

I had not told either of my brothers of my financial discoveries today, nor did I plan to. No, that was a little nugget I planned to keep to myself.

"They're meeting tomorrow night," I filled everyone in. "At The Roost. Five PM."

"And the organizers?" my father demanded in what was little more than a growl.

"Are you planning to fire them?" I questioned.

"First thing in the morning," he bellowed.

"You know, some of your employees have families," I countered. "Did you ever think about that?"

"What about *my* family?" My father's eyes narrowed as he looked from me to my mother and then to Clem and Carson. "I have to take care of my own family, you know. If my employees are having a hard time taking care of their families, maybe they should do what I did: work their asses off and start their own damn companies. Then they can call their own shots and find out how fucking hard it is to succeed. How much sacrifice it takes."

I said nothing.

No one said anything, as a matter of fact.

"I expect you to hand over a list of everyone involved by eight AM tomorrow," he finally said, setting his fork down on his plate and placing his napkin on the table. Then he scooted his chair back and stomped off toward his office.

I was too keyed up to eat. I glanced at my mother, silently requesting her permission to be excused, and then I fled the dining room, not stopping until I was behind the wheel of my old beat-up truck. Marcus's truck.

I wasn't sure what I was going to do now. I had managed to burn my bridge with Colleen, and then Jolie too. She probably wouldn't believe my real reasons for kissing Ellie in the gift shop. Hell, she didn't even know my real identity. It was beyond too late to fix that.

Or was it?

JOLIE

"I thought I could. I thought I could. I thought I could. I thought I could. I thought I could. I thought I could."

My words became faster and softer as I tried to make myself sound like a train chugging off into the distance. I closed *The Little Engine That Could* and glanced down at River, who had fallen asleep already. His little dark head was nestled against the pillows, and he wore such an adorable look of innocence on his face. He truly looked like an angel.

I was glad I got to spend a few minutes with him tonight, though I was hoping we had longer together before he drifted off to sleep. All the drugs they were pumping him full of made him so tired. That and helping him with his homework the school sent over completely drained the poor kid.

Only a couple more days of this, and he'd be back home. And after tomorrow night's press conference, things would start returning to normal. Or maybe they wouldn't. Maybe I'd be famous, and River's medical bill problems would be solved, and I'd be offered a role in the latest Hollywood blockbuster.

Hey, it doesn't hurt to dream.

I was going to stay with him a few minutes longer until I was sure he was sound asleep, and then I had to get to my appointment with Mr. Barry. I'd canceled last week, and he made it pretty clear if I continued to cancel, he was going to find a new Domme.

I needed the five hundred dollars a month he paid me. It made me sound like a horrible mother to leave my son in the hospital alone while I went to spank some old dude, but I was, in fact, doing it for the aforementioned son. For both of my sons, really.

I was wearing my usual BDSM attire, a black latex corset, under a loose-fitting dress. I'd have to put on my lace-up boots in the car. Getting into the corset by myself wasn't really an option because I could never lace it tight enough. My mother always had to help me get ready before I left the house.

My life was complicated. And a little weird.

I stood up, taking one more look at River before turning toward the door. My blood began to boil when I saw a familiar dark head poking his way in.

"Marcus!" I had to stop myself before I screamed and risked waking River up. "What the—what are you doing here?" I did manage to keep myself from using the F word, but only barely.

"Jolie, we need to talk." He pushed his way inside the small, sterile room and glanced around. His gaze fell on my son, who was hooked to a variety of tubes and monitors.

"I have nothing to say to you," I hissed, crossing my arms over my breasts.

His gaze lifted from the bed to meet mine. "Is this your son?"

I scoffed. "Yeah, one of the things I was going to tell you today after work, but you didn't show up. Instead, you chose to spend your time with Ellie in the gift shop."

"It's not what you think," he told me. "Nothing about me is what you think. That's why we need to talk."

"I have to go." I began to walk toward the door. "That means you need to go too."

"Where are you going?" He followed me out the door and down the hall.

"It's none of your business," I assured him as I pressed the elevator button. A nurse gave me a nasty glare as she passed, but I ignored her. I was sure all the nurses and doctors around here thought I was a tramp and a horrible mother, but I didn't give a flying fuck what they thought. All I knew was I was doing the best damn job I could.

Marcus climbed into the elevator after me even though I was shooting daggers at him from my eyes. Then he followed me out the automatic hospital doors, all the way to my car. I didn't say one single word to him the entire trek. The Floridian heat and humidity were sucking out my will to live, and my patience for dealing with bullshit had reached its rock bottom.

I whirled around to face him. "I have to go. I have another commitment." The last word was more of a sneer.

He grabbed me by the waist, and his eyes jerked up to meet mine. "What are you wearing under here? You're still wearing your corset?" He peered into my car. "Where's the rest of your costume?"

His eyes fell on the thigh-high black latex boots in my back seat and my black bag that carried all my implements: whips, riding crops, restraints, paddles, etc. It was a veritable BDSM arsenal in there. I couldn't imagine how shocked he'd be if he were to open that bag.

Remaining completely silent, I waited for him to start making some connections. Yeah, he wasn't the only one who wasn't as he appeared. This was why I shouldn't have gotten involved with him in the first place. Between my sons and my dominatrix gig, there was just no room for a normal relationship with a normal guy. Not even a hot, nerdy Brit with a beard and glasses.

"Jolie, what's going on?" His dark eyes bored into me as I unlocked my car door. It was so old that the key fob didn't work anymore.

Once I unlocked all four doors, I reached into the back seat to grab my boots. I was running out of time to get to the dungeon where Mr. Barry was waiting for me. Still refusing to answer Marcus's question, I plopped myself down in the driver's seat and took off my flip flops.

"Are you going to answer me?"

I glanced up and found a pleading look on his face, bordering on desperate. I huffed out a sigh. "I'm a professional Domme, okay? I have an appointment with a client I need to get to. So, if you'll excuse me..."

A groove between his eyebrows appeared as his gaze darted across my face, down to my boots and then back up again.

Well, I'd done it now. As if he wasn't already put off by my having a sick child, I was sure my dominatrix gig would be the straw that broke the camel's back. He wanted me to be The Red Velvet Queen, not Mistress Magenta. And certainly not the real Jolie Cox.

But why did I care? It wasn't like I had feelings for him—*Ugh.*

Okay, I did have some feelings. Otherwise, why did it sting so bad to see him kissing Ellie in the gift shop earlier today? Why would I care what he thought of my kids or my second job if I didn't have some semblance of feelings for him?

"What time is your appointment?" he asked. Not at all what I was expecting him to say.

"It's in fifteen minutes," I answered. "And I can't be late. I'm about to be fired."

He looked off into the distance for a second before glancing back to me. "How much does he pay you?"

"What?" I laughed. "What difference does it make? It's none of your business how much he pays me!"

He set his lips in a firm line as he drew in a deep breath, making his nostrils flare. "Whatever he pays you, I'll pay you double if you just cancel your...whatever you call it...and have dinner with me."

I couldn't help but burst into laughter. "What the fuck, Marcus? You think you can just buy my good graces after I caught you kissing another girl? I know we never agreed to exclusivity...but for fuck's sake, you're messing around with two women at work? Not very smart. Especially since she and I are friends."

He shook his head. "Like I said, that wasn't what it seemed. I was just trying to acquire some information. I can explain soon, I promise."

I didn't respond to that. I was still trying to wrap my head around how I got into this situation. *Oh, yeah, by thinking with my pussy instead of my brain. That's how.*

"Just tell me how much. I'll give you double," he reiterated.

"On your salary at Sweetopia? You can't afford me." I rolled my eyes. "My clients pay me five hundred a month."

"I can give you a thousand cash tonight." He crossed his arms over his chest.

"Right." I looked him up and down. He was a kid in his mid-twenties. A foreign exchange student, basically, a recent college grad who hadn't even nailed down a full-time job yet.

"I can give you..." He pulled his wallet out of his back pocket and took out a wad of cash, which he began to count.

I ripped the wallet out of his hand when I saw all the gold and platinum credit cards tucked into their slots. I flipped it over and glanced down at his driver's license, which looked to be a regular Florida one.

I was expecting to see the name *Marcus Young*, but that was not at all what appeared on the card.

Cyrus Anthony Sweet.

That was the name on his driver's license.

A sensation I hadn't experienced since the morning I woke up and River's dad was gone, leaving nothing, no note and none of his possessions behind, welled up in me like magma rocketing up a volcano. It was a burning, searing pain, ripping through my gut and funneling every bit of fear, anger, and hurt I had floating around in my body into one whirling, twirling cylinder of rage.

"Jolie, I can explain—" He reached out for me, but I slapped his arm away.

"Don't fucking touch me!" I hissed as his eyes filled with what looked like a mix of hurt, frustration and desperation.

I didn't even finish putting on my boots. After dropping the wallet into his waiting hands, I threw the second boot in the back seat and swung my legs into the car. I wanted to scream obscenities, but I couldn't even look at him.

I started up my car, slammed my door, and squealed out of the parking lot. I had no idea if he walked away, or if he was still standing there holding his wallet and trying to figure out who the hell he actually was.

Not only that, I didn't fucking care.

sixteen

CY

I didn't know how long I stood in the parking lot after Jolie drove off in a huff. I couldn't blame her. Yes, she'd hidden her second job and her son's health from me, but that was nothing compared to me pretending to be an entirely different person. A different nationality, even.

Her secrets were, well, completely understandable. They weren't the type of things you'd tell someone you barely knew. They were things you told someone once you'd gotten to know them a little. Those were probably the things she was planning to tell me earlier today when I was supposed to meet her in her dressing room after our shifts ended. And I would have been there to hear them if Colleen hadn't called me into her office.

Colleen. I needed to speak with her. Now wasn't the time to dwell on how badly I'd fucked things up.

I definitely had. No doubt about it.

But there was only one way I could get back in Jolie's good graces, and that way started by talking to my boss.

It only took me a few minutes to hack into the employee database to find her address and phone number. I thought about calling first, but I figured there was little chance she would answer, let alone invite me over.

I didn't know much about Colleen's personal life, but when I pulled up to her house, some things became clearer. She lived in a modest ranch-style brick home with two palm trees in the front yard. There was a "welcome" flag flying on the porch and a couple of Adirondack chairs painted bright teal.

Taking a deep, bolstering breath, I marched up the rock-lined walkway to her front door and rang the doorbell. I had ditched my glasses and would forgo the accent too. No need for those things now.

A teenage girl with a confused look on her face opened the door. "Hello?"

"Are you Colleen's Neese's daughter?"

A funny, embarrassed smirk appeared. "Yes?"

"Is your mom home? I need to speak with her."

She stood there for a moment, confusion still wrinkling her brows.

"I work with her at Sweetopia," I explained.

"Just a sec." She disappeared down the hallway, and in moments, she was replaced with an older, more filled-out version of herself.

"Marcus?" Colleen huffed out. "I mean Cy."

No pretense or subterfuge here. I was sure the desperation in my eyes and voice conveyed my true feelings. "Hey, can I come in? I want to talk to you."

She pursed her lips and reluctantly swung the door open. "What do you want?" she asked as she guided me into a small parlor off the foyer. She gestured to the loveseat as she took the armchair across from it.

"Is everything okay?" a tall, gray-haired man with a deep voice asked from the entryway once I got settled.

I stood up and extended my hand to him. "I'm Cy Sweet."

"Oh. Right," he said as if he'd already heard this story. He turned to his wife. "You okay?"

"This is my husband, James." She gave the man a pointed look as if to say she wasn't impressed by his lack of introduction. "I'm fine, honey. This won't take long."

"I just got back from talking to Jolie at the hospital," I started.

"What? How did you—"

"I called all the area hospitals till I found the one that had admitted a River Daniels."

She rolled her eyes. "Does the word 'privacy' mean anything to you? I'm surprised they gave out that information."

"Using a British accent and adding M.D. to your name really seem to help." I'd learned Jolie's son's last name from hacking into the employee information database at work. Same place I found Colleen's address.

"So why are you here?" She folded her arms across her chest and glared at me. Her expression was nearly as intense as it was earlier in her office.

"I want to help her," I explained. "I just found out she has a second job. And I know the issue she has with my parents and her benefits at work. I just want to help. Monetarily."

"You rich people are all alike," she seethed. "You think you can just sweep in and drop some cash on a situation, and it will fix everything. It's so fucking cocky."

I couldn't refute her accusation. But money *could* solve a lot of problems—if that wasn't the case, then why would Sweetopia employees be organizing this protest? They wanted more money, better benefits, and they were willing to strike and call for a boycott to get them. Those things would deprive my family of money. It was all about money. It always was. And always would be.

"Why don't you talk to your parents and get them to change their policies?" Colleen suggested. "Why don't you get them to make some changes before the media gets involved and there's a strike and boycott, and they're made to look like assholes, probably on national TV? Maybe even international…"

I considered what she said. I had tried to talk to my parents at the dinner table. My father was pretty sure he was the victim in this scenario, and I was beginning to see how pigheaded he was. How selfish.

Before going undercover boss in Sweetopia, I'd never thought of my parents as anything but hardworking, honest businesspeople. But they clearly had even more wealth than I could have ever fathomed and had used some questionable tactics to grow and maintain it. Meanwhile, their employees were suffering, being treated unfairly.

There was no reason my parents couldn't stay rich and successful *and* be fair to their employees. But I highly doubted they were going to listen to me if I suggested a compromise. No one in my family listened to me about anything. I was the baby. The party boy. The irresponsible one.

The Sweetopia employees were the ones who had the numbers, the voice and the plan. I wanted to see if there was a way I could empower them to be heard. They would have an easier time swaying my parents than I ever could—because they could hit them right where it hurt: their bank accounts.

"I tried to talk to them tonight at dinner." I rolled my eyes. "It didn't go too well."

"Then talk to your brothers; get them on your side," she suggested. "Look, Cy, if you want to make this better…if you want to help Jolie, you need to put in the work. Try harder. Money doesn't solve everything, you know. Step the fuck up, Cy."

"She knows now," I blurted out. "She knows who I really am."

Colleen's eyes widened as she stared at me. "And how did that go over?"

I sighed. "About as well as you'd expect. She really does hate my family, doesn't she?"

Colleen smirked as she nodded. "I know she hasn't been at the park for too long, but they haven't treated her well. They've treated her like an object, like a fictional character, not a human being. And they've been completely unreasonable about her needing time off to care for her son. Not to mention the medical stuff that isn't covered under their cheap insurance policy."

My guts were all twisted thinking about what she'd gone through. "I didn't know about her son till today."

"Your parents did," she fired back. "Trust me."

That made me angry. *My parents have three sons!* How could they not be sympathetic to the plight of a single mother of two sons? Especially if one of them had a grave illness?

Colleen continued, "Jolie hoped that portraying The Red Velvet Queen would get her some visibility. There's talk about a movie, you know...a live action movie."

There had been animated films based on the Sweetopia characters for quite some time. Books first, of course. Then films. My parents had talked about a live action film, but, as far as I knew, they hadn't found a studio or director they wanted to work with. I couldn't imagine a more perfect Red Velvet Queen than Jolie, though. And I knew they were very happy with her portrayal. She was definitely a fan favorite—

the line outside the throne room to meet her was proof of that.

"So that's why she wanted to stick it out in her job," I realized, "despite the bad insurance and benefits."

"She feels like it could be her big break, and once she started organizing this protest—"

"So she *is* the mastermind," I interrupted.

I knew Jolie was headstrong, but she was so young and relatively new at the park. I figured the lead organizer was someone who had been around a while, a veteran. Someone like Colleen.

"Jolie has the passion, the drive, the personality," Colleen explained. "I have the experience. We make a good team. She hopes telling her story to the media will open a lot of doors for her—with Sweet Enterprises, and in general…maybe in Hollywood."

"I see." Truer words had never been spoken. Everything had begun to crystallize. I knew what my next steps were.

I glanced down at my watch to see it was nearing eight o'clock. There was no more that could be done tonight, but tomorrow I needed to pay a visit to our family lawyer and then to my brothers.

I thanked Colleen for her time and advice, then headed home. My heart ached for Jolie and her son. But I also clung to the hope that I could help.

Since I'd met her, I'd felt this undeniable urge to take care of her. At first, that took the form of bringing her to orgasm over and over again. Now that I'd seen her true self and how hard she worked to take care of her family, I realized she didn't have anyone to take care of her, to protect her. To be the arms that wrapped around her and held her tight. To make the promise that she'd never be alone, and all would work out in the end.

I wanted to be those arms. I wanted to make those promises.

And like Colleen said, I couldn't fix this by just throwing money at the problem. I had to roll up my sleeves and get to work.

I'd always been an underachiever. I had carefully curated my reputation as the spoiled party boy whose sense of entitlement was off the charts. But what no one realized was that I *did* know how to work hard—when it was something I really cared about, really had a passion for.

And Jolie ticked those boxes. I not only cared about her, had a passion for her...

I might have even fallen in love with her.

JOLIE

Cyrus Anthony Sweet. Are you fucking kidding me?

I made it through the session with Mr. Barry, then high-tailed it home to do some research. My laptop was a bit dusty, but I fired that baby up and typed "Cyrus Sweet" into the search engine. Hundreds of results appeared. Most of them were about how the youngest Sweet boy was a world-class partier. "World class" in that he'd been all over the damn world—on his parents' dime, no doubt.

"How was River tonight?" my mother asked from the doorway to my bedroom.

"Hey, Mom." I angled the laptop screen down to hide my search, though I wasn't sure why. Instinct, I guessed. "He was tired. We did his homework, and I read him a story, and that was about it."

"And your session?" She wore a concerned look on her face.

"It was fine. Just the usual stuff." I shrugged.

"What are you doing now? Shouldn't you be in bed?"

"Shouldn't you?" Sometimes it was hard to tell who was mothering whom around here.

"Your big meeting is tomorrow, isn't it?" She stepped a little further into the room. "Is everything set?"

I nodded. "Yeah, good thing I'm not working tomorrow. I can sleep in a little."

"Maybe looking tired and worn out is a better game plan?" She smiled in a way that made me think she was probably joking. She did have a point, though.

"Yeah, maybe." I forced a smile. "Are you coming?"

"Did you talk to Dr. Grimes about discharging River early so he can be there?" She didn't answer my question.

I shook my head. "No. He needs to finish out his tune-up, plus I don't want to expose him to all those germs. If you don't want to come with Reed, it's fine. You guys can stay here. I've got this."

"You seem upset. What happened today?" She paced toward my bed, where she sat down. It was abundantly clear she wasn't going anywhere until I spilled it. She could always tell when something was bothering me.

I huffed out a long sigh as I debated what to tell her. Then I remembered my search on the laptop. I could give her a pretty fast executive summary accompanied by a visual aid. "Remember that guy from work I was seeing? Marcus?"

My mother nodded, her face lighting up at the mention of his name. She was obviously hoping I would be seeing him again.

"Yeah, so, this is him." I turned the laptop screen toward her.

She got up, moving closer to inspect the photos. "Whoa… that's—"

"The Sweets' youngest son, yes." My face immediately went into my palm before I ran my fingers through my hair.

"But—"

"An undercover boss thing, I guess. I am pretty sure his parents sent him in to get close to me, to try to uncover the plot to organize the strike and boycott." I blew another breath out as the implications fully coalesced. "He never even liked me. He just wanted to out me to his parents."

"Wow. Honey, I'm so sorry." My mom's eyes were filled with sadness for me. "He seemed so nice. How did you figure it out? What did he have to say for himself?"

"He actually tracked me down at the hospital. I don't know how. Pisses me off that he would even try to do that." I shook my head, trying not to let the anger bubble up inside me again, but it was too late. I could feel rage spiking the blood in my veins.

"He offered to pay me double whatever Mr. Barry was paying me if I would cancel my session with him. When he whipped out his wallet, all the gold and platinum credit cards caught my eye. He's in his mid-twenties so he shouldn't have all those. I grabbed the wallet from him, and that's when I saw his driver's license. He's not even British!"

My mom made a *tsk-tsk* sound. "That may be the biggest travesty of it all!"

I couldn't help but crack a smile. "Yeah, you're probably right."

"So what are you going to do?" She patted the space next to her on my bed, and I plopped down on the mattress beside her. She put her arm around my waist and squeezed me to her body.

"I'm not going to work tomorrow, so I can't be fired." I laid my head on my mom's shoulder as I continued, "And even if they did fire me, that would just make things worse for them when I talk to the press. I'm going to do my thing tomorrow and hope for the best. Fuck the Sweets."

My mom's laughter filled the room, and for a moment, I worried it might wake Reed up. But it was too contagious, and in seconds, I was joining in too.

Fuck the Sweets, especially the youngest one.

seventeen

CY

One errand down, one to go. I parked in the staff parking lot at Sweetopia in my beat-up truck. My cover was blown with Colleen and Jolie, but I didn't want anyone else to figure it out. I was hoping Colleen had kept her promise not to tell anyone.

I used the elevator that required a key to get up to the corporate offices at the top of Cotton Candy Castle. I'd never realized how plush and luxurious things looked up here. I guessed after spending time in so many kitchens and storage rooms, nice stuff was starting to look swanky to me.

I breezed past Clem and Carson's secretary. She tried to stop me, not recognizing me in my Marcus Young get-up. With the pink polo on, I must have looked like any other park employee. I glanced over my shoulder at her and simply said, "They're expecting me."

Poking my head into Clem's office first, I announced, "Conference room. Now." Then I did the same thing at Carson's office.

My dad's office was just down the hall. I happened to know it was his morning to play golf, which meant he was out on the green, not here. The timing was perfect.

I settled in at the head of the table, the position where my father typically sat. The last time I was in this room was when the entire family nominated me to be the one to be the undercover boss. Oh, how things had changed.

Hell, I was supposed to be leaving for Greece in two days, and I had nearly forgotten all about that trip. If things went as planned, I would still be going. And if *all* my dreams came true, I wouldn't be going alone.

"What the hell is going on? Where's Dad?" Carson grumbled as he took a seat in one of the leather executive chairs.

"I thought you were supposed to be down in the bakery. What are you doing up here? You're going to blow your cover," Clem added.

"You're such a fuck-up, Cy. I knew you wouldn't be able to pull this undercover boss thing off." Carson folded his hands together on the surface of the desk and glared at me.

I looked from one brother to the other and cleared my throat. I had rehearsed this speech on the way over here, and I wasn't backing down. "How much do you like your jobs here at Sweetopia?"

Clem furrowed his brows. "Well, it's not bad as far as jobs go. It's not like we do that much."

"You do know that Dad is planning to retire and turn the park over to the three of us next year, right?" I continued.

Carson spoke up with his normal know-it-all attitude. "Of course we know. But I think you mean turn it over to me and Clem. I'm pretty sure you're getting written out of the will after the stunt you pulled."

"Both of you need to listen really closely to me," I said, leaning toward them. I took a deep breath before laying all my cards on the table. "The Sweetopia employees have arranged a press conference tonight at The Roost starting at five PM. One employee will be telling her story about unfair treatment and accusing our parents of some pretty heinous things, including not adhering to FMLA laws. She has a pretty compelling story about the terrible health insurance we offer employees too. Her son has cystic fibrosis and is in the hospital as we speak."

"Are you talking about The Red Velvet Queen?" Carson questioned. "You fucked her, didn't you?"

"Of course he did!" Clem laughed.

"It doesn't matter who it is." I could tell they were not taking me seriously—a problem that had been going on my entire life. No one took me seriously. I was just the baby. What did I know?

"This is not going to bode well for Mom and Dad," I warned them. "Or for us. We need to go to the press conference and offer to do everything in our power to help our employees. To make things right."

Carson rolled his eyes. "If they don't like working here, they are welcome to get other jobs. It's not like we're forcing anyone to work here. Do you know how many applications we had for The Red Velvet Queen when we let the old lady go?"

Old lady. Wow. What a fucking tool, I thought to myself. Did I used to sound like that? Had I changed?

"How many of those applicants would have made a good Red Velvet Queen?" I questioned. Their faces were blank. "How many would have made even a *passable* Red Velvet Queen?"

Neither of them said a word.

"I don't think you guys are taking this seriously enough. They are calling for a strike. And a boycott. There are a) not going to be any employees to run the park and b) no guests are even going to show up because, once the public finds out how we're treating a single mom with a terminally ill kid, they will refuse to support our company. Mark my words."

Clem ran his fingers through his dark hair before settling his gaze on me again. "Have Mom and Dad made an action plan? They know this is coming, right?"

"Of course they do," Carson retorted. "But this is *not* going to be a big deal. Dad's been talking to his PR guy, and he said there may be a few days of lower attendance, but it won't last. It's just a storm. It will blow over. Like every other storm that comes through here."

"I think you guys are underestimating Jolie Cox," I warned them. "She is going to tug at the heartstrings of every single person in Florida—in America—with her story."

"Just because she's tugged at your heartstrings doesn't mean anyone else is going to care." Carson delivered his snarky remark with a proud smirk, then looked toward our brother for his approval.

Clem nodded. "Besides, we have the scoop on Jolie Cox, anyway. Dad's PR guy has done a little digging into her past, and she has not one but two baby daddies, dropped out of college, had an arrest for possession when she was in her early twenties, and not only that—here's the real clincher, folks—she works as a professional dominatrix."

"How did you find that out?" I blurted, feeling my blood rush to the surface of my skin. I had only found that out myself the day before. My brothers knew this whole time? My parents knew?

"We've had her followed, how else? Dad knew there was a pretty strong possibility she was involved in this. Why do you think he placed you in the bakery down the hall from her throne room? He knew you would try to get in her pants. He put you close to her so you could shut her up. Too bad your loyalty is to some skank and not the family!" Carson bellowed.

"Fuck you," I shouted back as I stood to my feet. I didn't have to listen to this.

As I headed to the door, Carson shouted, "You better think carefully about who you side with on this, Cy. I know you're Mom's favorite and all, but Dad will cut you off so fast, you won't even feel it until you've bled out. He can drain every single one of your bank accounts in a heartbeat."

Clem added, "That must have been some damn fine pussy for you to betray your own family like this."

I wasn't listening to any more insults. I had better things to do, and number one on my list was protecting The Red Velvet Queen.

JOLIE

I couldn't deny that I was nervous. Seeing Colleen in the room when I entered helped, and then Buster and Ellie came into view as well. I still wasn't very happy about seeing Ellie and Marcus—*ahem, Cy*— together the other day, but it wasn't her fault. She didn't know I was seeing him. Dozens of other full-time Sweetopia employees filled the room, all ready to cheer me on as I went to bat for all of us.

Colleen and Buster had set up a table at the front of the room with a few chairs. We each had a bit of a story to tell. Buster had been discriminated against because he was gay. The Sweets warned him that he was not to interact directly with any of the park guests. Colleen was going to talk about how she'd been screwed out of a promotion to the administrative offices because of the time she'd taken off when her husband had surgery a few years before.

Almost everyone in this room had a story to tell about how the Sweets had personally affected them—and not in a good way. We were poised to paint the Sweets as a family-unfriendly company, despite making their fortune under the guise of a family-friendly amusement park. The irony was something both the press and the public were going to eat up, and I couldn't wait.

As I settled in my chair at the center of the table, I looked up to see my mother enter the room with Reed in tow. I hated the fact that River wasn't with her, but I couldn't see having him discharged early from the hospital or exposing him to all the germs that might be lurking here. Reed was holding something that looked like a tablet, and he approached the table where I was sitting with it gripped tightly in his small hands.

"Hey, Mom," he said, stopping right in front of me.

"Hi, baby, what's up? What do you have there?" I looked into my son's wide blue-gray eyes, hoping he understood how important this moment was, how I was doing all of this for him and his brother.

"Hey, Reed, how's it going?" Colleen asked and held her hand out for a high-five, and Reed quickly slapped it before smiling over to Buster, who waved and also asked for "five."

"Mom, Grandma got me this tablet so I can live-stream the conference to River in the hospital." He looked down at the tablet, pressed a few things, then held it up. "Say hi to Mom," he spoke into the microphone.

He turned it toward me, and sure enough, there was River in his hospital bed. I looked behind him and saw that my aunt, uncle, and two cousins and all their kids were standing there with him. They must have driven down from Fort Myers to be part of this.

With tears forming, I looked across the room to my mother, who had matching tears in her eyes. She had set all of this up so River could be part of the press conference, and so he wouldn't be alone at the hospital. His face was beaming with excitement. He loved being around his cousins.

"Hi, River! Oh my gosh, you have a full room there, don't you?" My gaze swept from my precious baby boy to all the smiling faces of my family members.

"We can't wait to see you on TV, Mom!" he cheered. "You're gonna be awesome!"

"Are you nervous?" my aunt asked, looking down into the camera on River's matching tablet.

"So nervous," I answered with a wave.

"You can do this," she said, and my uncle and cousins all cheered.

The room became a hustling bustle of reporters and cameramen as they set up the press conference. Someone from the Associated Press who seemed to be the head honcho came over to speak with me.

"Are you all ready to go, Ms. Cox?" the tall woman in a navy blazer and matching skirt asked. She wore a paisley scarf around her neck in shades of jade, navy and white.

"Yes, ma'am!" I nodded and gave her my biggest, most confident smile. Inside, my stomach was churning, and there was so much adrenaline coursing through my body, I could probably run a marathon. I took in a series of deep breaths, reminding myself how much easier that was to do when I wasn't wearing a corset.

"We're a go in three minutes," she told me, then turned to the reporter who was standing nearby.

I scanned the room again, which had filled up almost to capacity. I was grateful Buster's boyfriend allowed us to use this room at The Roost for our meetings. It was the perfect space to hold the press conference as well.

As my eyes passed over the faces of everyone in the audience, I realized I was subconsciously looking for Marcus. *Cy. Whoever the hell he is.*

Why did he have to turn out to be one of the Sweets? Life had played many cruel tricks on me during my short thirty-two years, but this was one of the most hurtful.

I had been running the film reel of all our time together through my head on repeat since our confrontation at the hospital last night. And I'd been looking at my phone all day to see if he would try to text or call. My phone was buzzing right and left with people affiliated with tonight's press conference, but there was nothing from Marcus.

Ugh, no matter how hard I tried to hammer into my brain that he was Cy Sweet, I couldn't quit thinking of him as Marcus, my sweet, nerdy Brit, the amazing kisser with magical oral skills. Part of me wanted to ask if we could just put all of our differences aside for a few moments so I could experience one parting orgasm delivered on the tip of his tongue, but that was out of the question.

Was anything we shared real? Was he just using me to get intel for his parents the entire time, or did he actually like me? Did he stalk me at the hospital to come clean about his identity? I didn't exactly give him a chance to explain.

I was torn between wanting the answers to my questions and never wanting to see him or think about him again.

But the latter was impossible and pointless to wish for. He'd wedged himself inside my heart, and there was no denying I fell for him. I could pretend I didn't fall in love with him all I wanted to, but that was one role I'd never be able to pull off.

The reporter looked at me and nodded before turning back to the camera. Someone else counted down with the last few numbers silent, and a hush fell over the room. I tried to listen to what the reporter was saying, but my mind was hopelessly caught in a loop of questions about Marcus.

Ugh. Cy.

I glanced down at the microphone in front of me, prepared to spill my guts into it while looking into the camera with all the charisma and persuasion I could muster. All of my pain and anguish over Cy breaking my heart needed to be funneled into this press conference.

Next thing I knew, the reporter was turning to me, indicating it was go time. I took a deep breath before letting the speech I'd rehearsed fly:

"I'm Jolie Cox, and my fellow employees of Sweetopia and I are gathered here today to inform the public of how Sweet Enterprises treats its employees. I'm a single mom, and my son has cystic fibrosis. He's not able to be here tonight because he's in the hospital undergoing treatment for CF, but his older brother Reed is here." I pointed to my baby boy, who was holding up the tablet to video me, and he beamed back.

"Throughout my tenure at Sweetopia, around six months now, I've had to miss eight days of work. They've threatened to fire me repeatedly, even though doing so would be in violation of the Family Medical Leave Act. In addition, I'm forced to sit in one spot for hours at a time in a very restrictive costume with only one one-hour break each day. Many times, I need to work overtime to accommodate the long lines of guests wanting to meet the character I portray in the park, which is The Red Velvet Queen. The Sweets do not pay an overtime rate for this extra time. I'm paid at my regular rate, which is only fifteen dollars an hour."

As soon as I revealed my hourly wage, gasps rose from the audience. The Associated Press lady I'd spoken with earlier signaled for me to keep speaking, so I did.

"I have to work a second job to pay my son's medical

expenses because the health care coverage I get through Sweet Enterprises is so abysmal. I had to meet a fifteen-hundred-dollar patient deductible, and our family has to meet a five-thousand-dollar deductible before insurance even kicks in. My son requires frequent doctor visits, hospital stays, and is on a number of prescriptions. I hit the threshold for the deductible in only a couple of weeks on the policy. I am also responsible for twenty percent of all the expenses we incur—"

My eyes darted to the back of the room when I detected a shuffle. Some of the security guards from the park were attempting to barricade the doors, and loud shouts echoed down the center aisle to where the cameramen were set up. As if I wasn't nervous and hyped up enough, a new rush adrenaline of surged through me, making my hands tremble as I tried to figure out what was going on.

"Just a moment." The reporter held up one finger, and the main camera turned from me to him. "There appears to be a struggle at the back of the room. Let me remind you that we're live at The Roost in East Naples, covering the press conference with Sweetopia employees who are accusing their employer of unfair labor practices, low wages, and insufficient benefits."

Pandemonium erupted as the doors burst open and a horde of people rushed in. I recognized Mr. and Mrs. Sweet, along with their sons Clem and Carson. One of the sons—I could never keep them straight—attempted to rush the reporter and take his microphone, but he was immediately tackled by two of the security guards.

My pulse raced as people bolted from their seats, some joining in the melee, and some scrambling for safety. My mother grabbed Reed by the hand and led him to the front corner of the room where the American and Florida flags stood side by side.

My heart thrashed against my ribcage when I glanced at the open double doors at the back of the room and watched Cyrus Sweet push his way through the crowd, making a beeline toward his father. Mr. Sweet was shouting at the reporter, spewing hateful words about me.

"Don't listen to this delusional woman!" Corden Sweet bellowed. "She's nothing but an unfit mother whose side job is spanking and whipping men for money. According to our records, her son doesn't even have cystic fibrosis. She's making all of this up to attack and persecute our family!"

I stood up, the rage inside me unable to be contained. I began screaming at the top of my lungs into my microphone, which was apparently still on. "How dare you accuse me of lying about my son's medical condition! He's in the hospital, and we can prove it. Come here, Reed."

My son walked toward me and handed me his tablet, which showed River in his hospital bed surrounded by my family. I held it up to the camera as gasps and murmurs rose from the press conference crowd. "You and the rest of your family can all go straight to hell as far as I'm concerned! We're calling for a boycott. If anyone watching this has made plans to visit Sweetopia in the future, please stay home. Please don't spend one cent supporting the family behind his horrible company with no compassion or morals!"

As I was speaking, a shouting match erupted between Cy and his father, then the security guards escorted all the Sweets out of the room. All except for Cy. He pushed his way through the remaining guards and Sweetopia employees, giving them a line on repeat, but with the crowd's rising volume, I couldn't understand what he was saying. Next thing I knew, he crossed in front of the table where our microphones were set up and made his way around the end, tapping Buster, who sat next to me, on the shoulder until he surrendered his chair.

Cy still had the scruffy beard but wasn't wearing the glasses. When he sat down in Buster's spot wearing a light blue button-down shirt rolled up to his elbows, the crowd's murmurs died down, and everyone took their seats, waiting to hear what he had to say.

"Is this thing on?" He tapped the microphone in front of Buster's chair. The sound carried through the PA system, so he smiled and glanced around at the crowd, then directly at me before he took a deep breath and began to speak.

"Good evening, I'm Cyrus Sweet, youngest son of Corden and Ophelia Sweet." Murmurs began to stir up again amongst the crowd, but when he continued, silence fell so everyone could hear his smooth, deep voice with its surprisingly regular American accent. "I spent the last few weeks on an undercover assignment in Sweetopia. Did you guys ever see that show *Undercover Boss*?" There were some nods and affirmative mumbles. "That's basically what I was doing.

"My parents wanted me to investigate who was leading the employee revolt. They were aware of talk about a strike and boycott, and they wanted to know who was behind it so they could fire them immediately. They actually bribed me to bring them the information."

More gasps and murmurs rose until Cy began speaking again, "During my time in The Bard's Bakery, I worked for Colleen Neese, who is seated down the table here. Jolie Cox, whom you've already met, worked down the hall from me. I learned a great deal about the park I didn't know previously, and I have to say that my eyes were opened to the way Sweetopia employees are treated. I believe the individual area managers, such as Colleen in the bakery and Buster Baxter in the arcade, do a phenomenal job. The problem lies with senior management—namely, my family."

Another round of gasps and shocked whispers began to rumble through the crowd. I couldn't believe what I was hearing. Cy Sweet was admitting his family tried to use him to cover up their poor treatment of employees? They'd planned to fire anyone who was insubordinate, and Cy was outing them?

Cy glanced out and offered a humble grin to everyone before continuing once more, "I first want to apologize to everyone at Sweetopia whom I deceived with my undercover mission. I truly never meant to hurt anyone. I didn't understand what it was like to be a Sweetopia employee until I saw how our policies affected my coworkers. I'm here tonight because I want to take a stand against these policies. I want to call upon my parents to reevaluate their salary structure and leave policies. I want to challenge them to go back to the drawing board where their health insurance is concerned and to shop around for a different carrier with better, more comprehensive plans, as well as lower premiums and deductibles."

As soon as he said those words, the crowd was on its feet, clapping, cheering and hollering. I looked over at Cy, who was eating up the crowd's response. He did a fist-pump and beamed as his eyes trailed over the faces of all the Sweetopia employees who had come out to support *me* and *my* attempt to stand up to The Man, otherwise known as Corden Sweet.

But he was stealing all my attention, wasn't he? This press conference was supposed to be my big break, and now I'd been relegated to the sidelines.

Besides that fact—it wasn't as though Cyrus Sweet really had any power at all. His parents were going to do what they wanted. I doubted they cared about their son's little publicity stunt.

I wasn't done fighting.

Rising to my feet, I took my microphone off its stand so I could drop a little truth bomb on my fellow employees. "Does anyone really think the Sweets are going to do a damn thing if we don't hit them where it really hurts: in their bank accounts? Does anyone really think anything is going to change without a strike and boycott of the park? What was it Thomas Jefferson said? 'The tree of liberty must be refreshed from time to time with the blood of patriots and tyrants.'

"My fellow Sweetopia employees, we must fight back against these tyrants. Yes, the Sweets are tyrants. And, yes, we'll have to make sacrifices and prepare ourselves to go without a paycheck, but we must stand our ground, or we won't see real change."

Cy stood beside me, also untethering his microphone from its holder. But instead of addressing the reporters and the crowd, he turned to me. "Jolie, I'm doing the best I can here. I support your efforts. How else can I show you I'm on your side?"

I didn't expect him to make this about me and him, but two could play at that game.

My sharp gaze pierced into him as I taunted, "Oh, I don't know, maybe by admitting you came on to me as part of your undercover mission? That you made me think you really cared about me, but you were using me to get information on the employee uprising?!"

"That's not true!" he fired back, his eyes glittering with emotion and possibly the beginnings of tears. The crowd moved to the edges of their seats, silent enough to hear a pin drop as they waited to hear what he had to say.

He took my hand into his and captured my gaze with his own. "I hated lying to you, Jolie. At first, I justified it because my parents were threatening to take away my inheritance if I didn't perform this task for them. If I didn't give up the names of the perpetrators. But when I saw how their employment practices affected you and other park employ-ees, I couldn't sit by and let them destroy so many lives.

"And I know it looks like I used you to glean information,

but, trust me, every second I spent with you was because I wanted to. Because I couldn't stay away from you…"

His voice softened as he lowered the microphone from his mouth and let his own truth bomb fly: "Because I was falling in love with you."

eighteen

CY

I sure as hell didn't mean for those words to come out in front of a room full of people, but, hey, at least I didn't shout them into the microphone. But it became apparent that everyone heard me when silence blanketed the room.

"'Was?'" Jolie choked out. "Past tense?"

"No…" I shook my head, then I set my microphone on the table and took hers from her hand, placing it next to mine. I didn't know what the crowd was doing. I didn't know if the cameras were still rolling and focused on us.

And I gave exactly zero fucks. All I cared about was proving to this beautiful goddess that every single moment I spent with her over the past few weeks was genuine, even if I'd been Marcus Young during our time together instead of Cy Sweet.

"No, Jolie, I came to the hospital last night to tell you, to come clean about who I am. I also planned to tell you about my feelings for you."

Her brows furrowed as though maybe she didn't believe me. So I doubled down my efforts. What did Colleen say about needing to put in the work?

I took both of her hands into mine and squeezed. "Look, I didn't have a choice about going undercover. My parents and brothers didn't think I'd been pulling my weight with the family business, so they told me to accept the mission, or I was fired from the company—and the family. So, I did it. I had no idea you were involved in the Rebel Alliance—or whatever you want to call it—"

"Was that a *Star Wars* reference?" One corner of her lips tilted into a half-smile. "I mean, that's what we call our group behind the scenes—and it was *totally* a *Star Wars* reference."

"Why, yes, yes, it was," I fully admitted, a smile stretching my lips into a wide grin.

"So, you really are a nerd then?" she questioned with hope shining through her voice. "That wasn't part of your Marcus Young persona?"

"Oh, I'm definitely a nerd." I nodded adamantly. "I didn't make any of that up. I don't need glasses, but I sure do love me some Renaissance art, sci-fi movies, archaeology, astronomy and Monty Python. And Harry Potter and *Lord of the Rings*, and—need I go on?"

She laughed, her eyes crinkling with amusement. "Is it bad that makes the lying about your identity thing a hell of a lot easier to swallow?"

I squeezed her hands in mine again. "I don't really have a British accent either, as you may have noticed…though I do actually speak French. The British thing was part of my disguise, but I can certainly reprise it on occasion if you want. Maybe as a special treat?"

She looked down at our entwined hands for a moment, and when she looked back up at me, a tear glimmered in the corner of her gray-violet eyes. She pushed her shoulder-length hair behind her ear. "You really do like me like this? Like Jolie Cox? Single mom, actress-wannabe and dominatrix on the side?"

"Well, we may need to talk more about that side gig, but abso-fucking-lutely," I whispered back. "Can you handle that I'm not a poor college grad from London with severe myopia?"

"Well, you're going to be poor now if your parents disown you, aren't you?" she joked, a little laugh spilling out of her mouth.

"Maybe," I admitted with a shrug.

We had an entire audience hanging on our every word, and I had no idea if the news cameras were still rolling. But I didn't give a single fuck. I had to know.

I leaned in, my lips lingering near her ears. "Tell me...are you falling in love with me too?"

She pulled back, straightened her shoulders and fixed her gaze on me. "I wanted to deny it. I kept telling myself my feelings weren't real and didn't matter. All that mattered was taking care of my kids. I even tried to tell myself I was selfish for wanting something for myself..."

"But?" Never before had so much hope clung to a single syllable.

"But I want to see where this goes," she gestured between us, "because I can't stop thinking about you. Trust me, I've tried."

I laughed as I watched her emphasize the word "tried," her face lit up with animation.

"Even after I found out who you really are," she continued, "I still want you. And not for your family's money, Cy. I want to make sure you understand that. The man I fell in love with was a recent college grad with a temporary summer job at a family theme park. I don't expect anything beyond that."

I smiled at her, still oblivious to what was going on in the rest of the room. "I have a surprise for you outside. Will you come with me?"

"Are we done here?" Her eyes finally broke their focus on me to glance around the room. The Sweetopia employees were cleaning up, folding tables and chairs. The press was putting away its equipment. "Did we miss it? The rest of the press conference?"

A middle-aged lady who looked uncannily like Jolie bounded up toward the stage with a little boy who was carrying a tablet. "What happened?" Jolie asked her.

"It's over. They interviewed Colleen and Buster, and then the press conference finished up. I think they had to go back to the local news," the woman explained.

Jolie wrapped her arm around my waist. "Mom, this is Cy Sweet. Cy, this is my mother, Felicia Cox."

I extended my hand. "Nice to meet you, Ms. Cox."

"Please, call me Felicia. So what did the security folks do with your parents and brothers?" she questioned. "Did they get thrown out?"

"No idea. Let's go find out!" I gestured toward the open aisle and noticed others were starting to filter into the restaurant. We were set up in the back room reserved for parties and receptions. The dinner crowd was still thick, especially for a weeknight.

I wondered how many dinners were ruined when my family busted their way through the restaurant and into the private room. It was another item on a long list of ways my family had embarrassed me. But at least I did something to stand up for Jolie and the other Sweetopia employees. It wasn't enough, not yet, but it was a start.

And I had more tricks up my sleeve.

Jolie tugged on my arm to stop me before we exited the

room. "Cy, this is my son Reed," she said, her hands on the young boy's shoulders. "Say hi to Mr. Sweet."

"Hi, Mr. Sweet," Reed parroted before holding up the tablet so I could see it. "This is my brother, River."

"Hi, River!" I waved at the little boy in the hospital bed. The boy and the crowd surrounding the bed all waved back.

"Hey, I just saw you on TV!" the little boy exclaimed, his blue eyes gleaming. He had pale skin and dark hair, darker than his mother's, but I could definitely see he had her nose and lips.

"We're going outside for a few minutes," Jolie told River. "But after we finish up here, we'll come over to the hospital, alright?"

"Okay, Mommy!" A grin tugged up the corners of his mouth.

My heart ached for that little boy in the hospital bed. I was glad he was surrounded by so many loved ones, but I felt terrible about the horrible disease he lived with, the disease that would someday claim his life unless a cure was found. Jolie reached down and grabbed my hand, sending a jolt of electricity up my arm. It eased the pain I felt for the little boy on the screen, but it could never take it away.

I'd never thought about having children of my own. Probably because, a few months ago, I was still acting like a child myself. This experience—it had changed me. I couldn't explain why, but I felt this overwhelming desire to take care of that little boy in the hospital bed, his brother, and definitely the beautiful woman they called Mom.

I led the group out and around the side of the restaurant to where the deck began. It was a long, elevated structure that overlooked the inlet below that flowed into Naples Bay. Its wooden posts were surrounded by reeds and cattails, and we could hear the locusts and frogs starting up their evening concert.

"I'm just going to run to my car and get something, and I'll be right back, okay?" I asked. "Can you and your family wait for me on the deck?"

Jolie nodded. I watched her whisper something to her mom before the older woman and the young boy followed her down the path toward the steps to the deck. I headed over to my '69 Camaro—boy, it was great to be driving it again—immediately noticing a small crowd had gathered around it.

My family. Go figure.

"What do you guys want?" I shouted across the lot as I approached my car.

I could tell from their angry glares that I was about to be on the receiving end of a whole lot of bullshit, bullshit I wasn't in the mood to deal with currently.

"Do you mind? I need to get something out of my car, and then I'm needed elsewhere." I shoved the key into the lock and twisted it.

"What the hell is wrong with you?" my dad bellowed, coming around the car to focus his wrath directly at my face.

"I can't believe you betrayed your family like that, Cyrus," my mother added. "I thought we raised you better than that."

"I can't believe you tried to defame a struggling single mom of a terminally ill child on television," I sneered to my father.

"She's an actress, Cy!" Carson shouted. "Get a fucking grip!"

"You know she's fired, right?" Clem pointed out.

I ignored them for a second, reaching into my car to grab a manila file folder full of documents I'd been collecting during all my errands earlier in the day. I shut my car door, locked it, and swiveled around to face my family.

"Here," I handed a document to my father, "this is a statement from the family attorney about my trust fund. Maybe you didn't realize that, when I turned twenty-one, you no longer had any control over the account, but you've officially been taken off the register for it."

"What? You can't—" my father began to protest.

"Trust fund? What?" Clem spoke up. "Don't we have trust funds too?" He elbowed his brother, who joined in the complaint.

"Also, here's the business card for the woman I spoke to at the district office for the U.S. Department of Labor. She's going to be in touch with you soon to address some of the concerns I brought up as well as the ones uncovered by the press conference tonight. And I think you'll have plenty of time to iron things out with her because there's going to be a massive strike at Sweetopia, along with a boycott. So you won't have anything else to do besides cooperate with their investigation."

My mother huffed when I handed the card over to my father. "What else is in there?" She eyed my folder, which contained more documents.

"Oh, those are my boarding passes. For the flight I'll be on tomorrow to Greece. Have fun cleaning up this huge mess you've created!"

The four of them all opened their mouths to speak, but I didn't stick around to hear what they had to say. I had better things to do. So I tucked my folder under my arm and headed back to where my queen was waiting for me.

JOLIE

It took Cy—I was finally getting used to calling him that—so long to return to the deck that I was beginning to wonder if he was coming at all. I had been burned by so many men that learning to trust him was going to be a challenge for me, especially after the whole Marcus Young undercover boss fiasco. But I wanted to try. My head kept reminding me to be cautious, but my heart, and oh, you know, a couple areas further south were all about giving him another chance.

What he said about feeling powerless when his family pressured him for the info on the Sweetopia rebels resonated with me. I understood the feeling of powerlessness. Of help-lessness. When what was at stake really crystallized, he found his power. His strength. And he was willing to walk away from his family fortune to do right by me and the rest of the Sweetopia employees. I had a lot of respect for that. So of course I had to give him another chance.

"Hey, sorry, my family was stalking me back at my car." Cy's eyes swept across the bench we were sitting on, facing the water. Reed was focused on a beautiful white egret wading into the marsh with the tall green grasses behind serving as a gorgeous backdrop. He pointed it out, and my mother smiled at Cy before turning her attention to her grandson and the bird.

Cy reached for my hand and lifted me off the bench. "I'm going to just steal her for a minute, okay?" he asked Reed and my mother politely.

They both nodded, still entranced by the bird, so I followed Cy over to the railing that separated the deck from the water. The sun was sinking toward the inlet, casting an orange glow on the marsh. "Wow, it's really gorgeous out here, isn't it?"

"Stunning," he answered, "but not as stunning as you."

"Oh, so I see the cheesy flirts weren't just reserved for your Marcus persona, huh?" I looked up at him, enjoying the easy grin that spread across his face when I teased him.

"Nope. I'm as nerdy and cheesy as they come." He took

my hands into his. "And right now, I really want to kiss you…"

"Just a minute…" I raised my finger. "I just want to make sure, again, that you're okay with all this. That I'm older. That I'm a mom. That I am now jobless." I laughed at the last part. What else could I do at this point? I knew getting fired was probably a foregone conclusion when I started organizing the strike and boycott. "I guess you're jobless now too, huh? Wanna head for the unemployment office with me tomorrow?"

"That won't be necessary." The easy smile never faltered as his eyes bounced between mine.

"Oh, yeah? Are you independently wealthy too?" The cool evening breeze coming off the inlet blew my hair into my face, and I wrangled it away and behind my ear.

"Something like that," he said. "It's a trust fund. But it's all mine."

"So…you're not poor?" I squinted at him as I waited for his answer. It didn't matter to me either way, but having money was always better than not. I'd been poor enough of my life to know that.

"Not at all." He chuckled as he reached into his back pocket. "As a matter of fact, I'm leaving for Greece tomorrow."

"Oh, yeah, that's right. I thought maybe that was part of the act." I couldn't help but feel a bit of disappointment that we'd have to put whatever this was on hold until he got back. Or maybe he was trying to tell me that this was it. He stood up for me and against his parents, but this was where the train stopped. This was where we all got off.

"No. Not part of the act. I'm supposed to go and study sculpture with this brilliant artist and archaeologist." He shrugged. "Like I said, the nerd thing is for real."

I laughed. "So it is. That's a relief!" He was letting me down easy, wasn't he?

He turned over the papers he'd pulled out of his pocket. "But I want you to come with me."

The boarding pass he held out toward me had my name printed on it.

What. The. Fuck? Was this guy for real?

I'd been asking that question all along.

"I…I can't do that. I mean, I have—"

"Well, you don't have work at Sweetopia," he reminded me with a smirk.

"No, but I have clients…and my sons, of course…"

"Hey, Felicia," Cy called over my shoulder to my mother. "Hi, sorry for interrupting, but can you come over here for a minute?"

My mother smiled and made her way over to the railing. Reed remained on the bench, now fascinated by something on the tablet. "What can I do for you?" she asked as she stopped by my side.

"Jolie has the chance to go on a two-week, all-expenses-paid trip to Greece," he explained. "Do you think she should go?"

"What? Two weeks?! I can't be gone for two weeks!" I protested, looking toward my mom for back up.

A smile crept across my mother's face as the fading sunlight rained down on her aging features. "I think you should definitely go to Greece for two weeks," she said firmly, like she didn't even need to think about it.

"But River is still in the hospital, and—"

"River gets discharged in two days," my mother reminded me. "And we will be just fine for two weeks."

"But I've never been away from my boys for more than one night!" I continued to argue.

I could tell Mom and Cy had developed an instant

rapport, because all he had to do was beam his smile and dark eyes in her direction, and she was obviously smitten with him.

"I think that's all the more reason for you to go to Greece, Jolie. It's not like you don't have a passport." My mom shrugged as she soaked in Cy's happy wink.

It was true. I had a passport from when I took the boys to Niagara Falls last summer.

"But he wants to leave tomorrow." It was my last shot at talking some sense into the woman.

"Sounds great to me," she said, grinning. "Let's stop by the hospital to see River, and then you can go pack."

"I really like your mom," Cy announced, squeezing my hand and giving my mother another wink.

"Great, just what I need is the two of you ganging up on me!" I rolled my eyes as they both just laughed.

"I'll be over there with Reed while you two finish up this discussion. Let's not wait too much longer to get to the hospital, though, or River will be asleep," she reminded me.

"Good point." I watched her take her seat next to my son, then I shifted my gaze back to this handsome man in front of me. Even without glasses and his sexy British accent, he was still pretty fucking hot. *I'd do him.*

"So, you'll come with me?" he asked again. "I know it's short notice. I know we barely know each other...but I bet you we'll know each other a hell of a lot better by the time we come back."

I scoffed. "Yeah, no kidding. What are the sleeping arrangements?"

He grinned. "Well, if I get my way, it will be naked in one bed...but I think the condo I rented has two bedrooms." He trailed a finger down my cheek. "I feel like I've just barely scratched the surface of your body in the time we've spent together thus far..."

"Same," I retorted. "But I've gotta warn you, I'm a bit of a freak…"

"Well, you are a Domme," he conceded.

"Yet I had no issue with you dominating me." I shrugged. "You definitely bring out a side of me I'd like to explore a little bit more… Maybe I'm a switch after all?"

"So…is that a yes to Greece, then?" His dark eyes blazed with hope.

I flung my arms around his neck. "Yes to Greece. Yes to a kiss. Yes to it all!"

That was all the affirmation he needed. He wrapped his arms around my waist and pulled me in for the sweetest kiss I've ever received.

No pun intended.

epilogue

JOLIE

Holy shit, Greece was, in one word: epic. Hot days, cool nights, the breeze coming off the water was like a bevy of goddesses all fanning you with palm fronds. While Cy studied with the sculptor all day, I did something I hadn't done in forever: relax.

So far I'd gone to the spa, gone shopping, laid out on the beach—even the topless beach. I felt so free and uninhibited here. It was truly paradise.

And the sex…

Well, here was what happened last night:

Cy bought me some silk scarves at the market. I thought he might have some ulterior motives, which were proved when he asked if he could tie me up.

"You're not the one used to being tied up, huh?" he asked with a devilish gleam in his eyes. It looked like he had been thinking about this moment for a long time.

"Uh, no…" I answered with a head shake. "And what

exactly are you planning to do to me after you tie me up? If I indeed grant you permission to do so, of course."

He smirked as his eyes trailed up and down my body. He seemed pretty confident that permission would be granted. We had just come in from the beach, and I'd taken a quick shower, throwing my hair into a messy bun and slipping on a gauzy white dress with nothing underneath. This was the longest I'd gone without wearing a corset in months. My body was enjoying the ability to breathe freely.

"That's for me to know and you to find out," he quipped as he licked his lips.

What a fucking tease!

"I don't plan to be gentle about it either," he warned me. He took the scarves off the table in our little kitchen and made his way toward me, taking long, purposeful strides. I hadn't said yes, but I hadn't said no either. I was still thinking about it.

He grabbed my wrist and tightened his fingers around it. Just his grip alone shot flames of desire right down into my core, flames that could only be extinguished by his talented tongue or his magical cock.

"This looks like a yes to me," he said as I arched my back in need.

"Yes…" I managed. My heart skipped a beat as he pulled my wrist up toward the headboard and quickly tied me to it. Then he rushed around to secure my other wrist. I lay there completely helpless, vulnerable to his every whim. After all, I said yes. I surrendered my power to him.

Might have been a big mistake.

He pulled at my dress. "Ah, now this I fucked up. I should have taken this off first."

I gave him a teasing smirk. "See, being a Dom isn't as easy as it looks, huh?"

"Well, we'll just rectify my error like so…" He grabbed

ahold of the hem of my skirt with both hands, and then like a lightning bolt striking, he tore it all the way up to my chest.

"What the fuck, Cy?! That was brand-new!" He'd bought me the dress at the market the same day he bought the scarves.

"I'll buy you another one. Right now, I need to see those breasts and that pussy." His eyes were veritably glowing with his sick, twisted thoughts. "You better be quiet now," he warned.

"Or what?" I loved challenging him. I was learning I wasn't a submissive as much as a brat. Overpowering me had become one of his favorite pastimes in the last few days.

He didn't answer with words but straddled my chest, his strong, muscular ass pressing down against my breasts as he fisted his swelling erection and pressed it to my lips. "Take my cock," he instructed. When I hesitated, he grabbed my head with one hand, tilted it back to expose my throat, and then plunged deep into my mouth, taking my breath away.

"That's better," he sighed as I began to suck him. He knew how much I loved sucking his cock—or trying to. It was a challenge to get more than a few inches into my mouth because he was so damn thick.

He spun around to give himself access to my body, then inched his way down it, feasting and nibbling on every point of interest along the way: my nipples, my navel and my hipbones. He was building up a huge wall of need, and he would build it sky-high before he allowed me to come. *If* he allowed me...

Sure enough, the teasing licks to my labia and clit ensued, him moaning and humming his pleasure as he went, only stirring up a greater need for release. He was going to take his time, make me wait for it. I didn't know how he did it, but he could bring me right to the edge but leave me hanging by a thread. Then, when my aching, writhing body stilled in defeat, he'd start the whole process again. I was pretty sure he qualified as a sadist.

"Cy…" I wanted so badly to fist his hair and pull his head back to my center. I was desperate to take what I needed to soar off the ledge he kept leaving me on. But I was bound, unable to move. It only intensified my need.

Desire ran so deep within me, it stretched and surged through my whole body. Every nerve was shredded to its last fiber. "I need you, please…"

"Please what?" he moaned as he pulled away from that tender, swollen button once more.

"Please let me come." I looked down until our eyes met, hoping he could see the desperation in them. "I need your cock."

I didn't want to come on his tongue, though it would have felt nice. No, I needed that deep, all-consuming satiation that could only be delivered by his massive cock.

"When do you want it?" He gave me a playful smirk before delivering a lick right to my clit, where he finished with a swirl and a tiny nibble, electrifying those shredded nerves all over again. Lighting them up like a Christmas tree.

"Now, baby, please?" Those were the only words I could muster.

He slid up my body as if he were the victor in an epic battle. His erection pressed against my thigh as I shifted my hips, desperately trying to move it toward my pussy. I could tell from the slow, lingering way he began to kiss my neck that he was going to make me work for it.

"Come on, please?" I was starting to get impatient. *Okay, fine, beyond impatient.*

"I love how badly you need me, Jolie," he whispered against my ear, sending a new batch of shivers up and down my spine. "You may be able to tell that I need you pretty badly as well…"

He said the last part in his Marcus Young British accent, and it almost made me detonate right then and there. *Holy shit, the power of an accent!*

When my body throbbed beneath him, I sensed a sticky wet spot on my thigh. He wasn't making it up. He was exercising as much restraint as he possibly could.

"But why? Why deny yourself?" I questioned. "Take me, and we can both have our fill."

"What a logical conclusion," he agreed with a chuckle. He reached down to grab his manhood, positioning it between my lips. "So, you definitely think I should head in this direction?"

My jaw clenched as the tip of his cock brushed against my sensitive clit. I couldn't manage much more than a grunt.

"Is this what you want, Jolie?" he asked again, sliding maybe a half-inch past my lips.

He untied me, and I immediately wrapped my arms around his waist, fingers digging into his firm, round ass cheeks. "Yes, please."

"More?"

"Yes, more." I pushed my hips up, trying to take more of him, but the fit was too tight. He always had to work his way in slowly, gradually, as much as I wanted to be filled by him in one swift thrust.

He seemed to lose his restraint when he slid the next inch into me. He pulled up onto his wrists, hovering over me, his jaw clenched in concentration. "Fuck!" he blurted out as he grabbed my hips and thrusted hard, causing me to cry out.

"Fuck, baby, I'm sorry—"

"No, just fuck me." It was overwhelming, not painful so much as it took my breath away. I didn't care now. I needed him. Any way I could get him.

"I think I've held back too long," he admitted. "I don't know how much more I have in me..."

"What else do I have to say? Just fuck me, dammit!" I growled.

That was all the encouragement he needed. He slid both hands underneath me, drawing my hips toward him as he began to pound into me with all the strength and speed he could muster. I held on for dear life, clutching him with my fingernails dug into his muscular back for stability. My hips began to move at the same speed, meeting him at the top of every thrust, taking him as deep as I could.

Whatever had started between us back at Sweetopia had reached full bloom in this brief excursion to paradise. I never thought I could surrender my heart to another man after everything that had happened with Reed and River's fathers. But Cy was…extraordinary. There was no other word for him.

Except maybe sweet.

And it was that sweet cascade into ecstasy that enveloped our intertwined bodies as we both found our release. Sweat beading, hips pumping, lips biting, muscles spasming as wave after wave of pleasure crashed over us.

This was paradise as much as Greece was. It was everything I always wanted but never thought I deserved. Cy called me his queen.

And I finally believed it.

CY

The moonlight painted the water with light silver strokes as the waves rolled toward shore. The view from the hot tub was perfect, and the company was even more perfect, if that was even possible.

"Do you know how I said back at the press conference that I was falling in love with you?" I asked Jolie as I stroked my fingers down the side of her damp cheek.

I watched the corners of her lips rise as she processed my question. "How could I forget?"

"Well, I think my feelings have changed," I told her, then watched those lips fall as fast as they'd risen.

"What do you mean?" I detected a hint of panic in her voice.

I squeezed her hand in mine and wrapped my other arm around her, bringing her into my embrace. "I mean it's no longer a 'falling' sort of proposition."

"It's not?" she whispered, her voice taking on a silvery edge like it was reflecting the moonlit waves.

"No, I'm pretty sure it's just…"

I wasn't going to beat around the bush here. I really wanted her to know how I felt. I turned toward her, taking her face into both of my hands as her eyes lifted to me. The moon was reflected in them, and I'd never seen a more gorgeous sight in my life.

"What, Cy?"

"I've never said this to a woman before," I admitted—and it was true. I'd never been able to see past my own selfish needs to truly put someone else above myself. But there was something about Jolie that made me want to be a better man, to be the man she deserved.

She smiled as if she knew what was coming, but she didn't say a word.

"I love you, Jolie," I breathed out before pressing a kiss to her forehead. "I never thought it was possible for me to feel this way about someone. I didn't even understand what being in love meant. But here I am, completely, utterly, desperately, madly in love with you."

Her lock on my gaze never wavered. "I'm still working on

trusting you. It's been so long since I've let myself feel much of anything except for the love I have for my mom and sons. But I do feel love for you, Cy… It's why I couldn't be as angry with you about the whole undercover boss thing as I should have been. I felt such a strong connection to you that I had to believe you felt it too—that it wasn't all an act—"

"None of what we did was an act," I assured her.

She laughed. "Yeah, now that I've gotten to know you better, I realize you're not really much of an actor…"

"Oh, is that so?"

A soft sigh fell from her lips. "Yeah, Marcus Young was pretty much Cy Sweet with a beard, accent and glasses. I just wish everything hadn't gone south. I wish we'd been able to work things out with your family. I actually think I'm going to miss that place—"

"Eh, we'll figure something out," I promised.

"Don't you miss your family?"

I shook my head. "No, not really. They're all selfish assholes…just like I was on my way to becoming —permanently."

"Maybe they'll redeem themselves someday?" Her tone had a hopeful edge to it.

"Maybe," I agreed. "But for now, I feel like I'm starting a new, better family…"

"Wow." She didn't seem able to say much more than that. And I couldn't tell if it was a good "wow" or a bad "wow."

As long as I was sharing, I might as well lay all my cards on the table. "As much as I love it here, I'm anxious to get back to Florida and get to know your boys and your mom. And work on talking you all into moving in with me—"

"At your condo?" Her eyes narrowed. "It would be a little cramped…"

"No, silly woman. Into the house I plan to buy with some of the money in my trust fund. I have a couple of properties in mind. I've been looking online a bit since we arrived." I watched her eyes light up as bright as the moon.

"Are you serious?"

"Super serious." I chuckled at her surprised reaction as I brushed a few strands of hair out of her eyes. "When I put my mind to something, I dive right in. Like I said, I love you. I want to dive in."

"I see." The words floated off her lips and hung there like little bubbles that might burst at any moment.

"Is that too much? Are you not ready to dive in?" I fought off the crack of worry in my voice but lost that battle.

She smiled as she took my hands into her own. "Nope, I'm ready." She breathed out. "Because I love you too. It's all new—and I'm not going to lie, scary as fuck—but I am ready to dive in too."

"We have a lot of good times ahead of us, Jolie." I settled back into the hot tub, stretching one arm over the side and the other around her shoulders as she nuzzled into me. "So many fun things to explore…"

She giggled softly but then stopped when another couple approached the hot tub. I'd almost forgotten there were other people staying in this building, it had been so quiet all week. The woman was a tall, statuesque blonde, and the man had long, lean limbs and a head full of thick black hair.

"Mind if we join you?" he asked.

"Of course," Jolie agreed, and the couple slipped down onto the bench across from us.

In the course of our small talk, we learned the woman was Katja and the man was Moon-Soo. She was from Finland, and he was of Korean descent, though he'd lived in the U.S. for most of his life.

"So what brings you to Greece?" I continued our small talk.

They curled up affectionately in the tub together, her

head resting on his shoulder, their skin colors contrasting beautifully in the pale moonlight. "Vacation," she answered. "We both work for the same tech company."

"Right," Moon-Soo agreed, "but it's been crazy there. They've had mergers, and we've both gotten promoted. It's really stressful, and some days we want to chuck it all and become entrepreneurs or something. You know, work for ourselves."

As much of an optimist as I was, I couldn't help but deliver a dose of pragmatism. "Entrepreneurship is hard too, though. It has its own challenges."

"What do you do?" Moon-Soo questioned. "It sounds like you're speaking from experience. You have your own business?"

I laughed, not really sure how to answer. "My family had a business."

"*Had?*" Katja interjected.

Jolie took my hand and squeezed it as if to tell me I didn't need to go into all the sordid details. "It's a long story," I explained, and my queen flashed me a reassuring smile.

"We've thought about just dropping everything, moving to some exotic island in the Pacific or Caribbean, and starting an adults-only resort," Katja said. "Clothing optional, you know?"

Jolie's ears perked up as fast as mine did. "That sounds fun," she agreed.

"So what was your family business?" Moon asked. "Maybe you could give us some advice?"

I laughed. "Oh, well, my family ran a theme park...you know, for kids. So I'm not sure it would have much—"

"Theme park!" Jolie's eyes lit up. "You guys should build an adult theme park instead of just a resort."

"Adult theme park," Katja echoed, rolling the idea around

in her mind. "That sounds like a blast. Original too. What do you think, Moon?"

He smiled as I shot Jolie a look. "Wouldn't you encourage people to stay out of the theme park business?"

She just shrugged and sat back with a sheepish smile.

Moon's brow crinkled as if he was in deep thought. "What was your theme park called?"

"Sweetopia," Jolie answered for me. "You may have heard about it on the news recently."

"Oh, wow, that was you guys?" Katja's gaze bounced between us.

"It was my family's park," I corrected.

"Sweetopia," Moon repeated, trying to make the connection.

"I still think an adult theme park would be amazing!" Jolie was apparently stuck on the idea. "Just think of all the different rides and…games…we could have. There could be a BDSM land. You'd be surprised how many people just want a good spanking." She laughed as she glanced around the hot tub. "And they'll pay good money for that shit."

"I wouldn't be surprised!" Katja replied, shooting Moon a wink.

"Yeah, okay," I went along with this crazy conversation. "So, not Sweetopia…but *Spicetopia*."

Jolie sat up straight. "Yes. Yes, that's exactly what it would be."

"That sounds brilliant!" Katja agreed.

"What? I'm just teasing." I waved my hand to dismiss their crazy ideas.

"No, Cy, it's perfect. Spicetopia," Jolie repeated. "We're totally doing this."

"We want in," Moon announced.

"An adult theme park," Katja repeated. "Brilliant."

Jolie grabbed my hand, making me turn to face her. "I'm super serious, Cy. Spicetopia. We need to do this."

"Really?" I couldn't help but be skeptical. What did I know about building a theme park?

Well, I knew a lot more than the average person, that was for sure. Maybe it wasn't such a crazy idea after all.

"Spicetopia," I said again. It was sounding less crazy every time I repeated it.

"Spicetopia," the three others echoed.

"We can totally do this, Cy," Jolie assured me. "One hundred percent."

"Alright." It wasn't as if I didn't have the knowledge and the capital to get this thing off the ground. "Let's do this. Spicetopia it is!"

Jolie slung her arm around my shoulder, drawing me toward her face. Her lips brushed against mine, and in the distance, I heard the waves crashing along the beach. We may have been tipsy, and the moonlight may have been filling our minds with crazy delusions, but I really did believe in that moment, with my queen by my side, I could do anything.

Even build Spicetopia.

Continue the Spicetopia Series in Book Two, Virtue & Vice.

Books2read.com/Spicetopia2

USA Today Bestselling Author Phoebe Alexander writes romance about characters like her: with extra curves and life experience. Her stories often include themes of ethical nomonogamy, such as polyamory. She believes love is love, and everyone deserves a happily ever after, no matter your size, shape, age, or color.

Phoebe lives near the beach on the East Coast with her husband and multiple fur babies. When she's not writing, she works as an editor and consultant for indie authors. She also volunteers to run a 6000-member indie author support group.

Phoebe enjoys hanging out with her three adult sons, as well as travel, Broadway musicals, dark chocolate, swimming, hiking, college basketball, and making Seinfeld references whenever possible, especially in her books. Her single greatest fantasy is just having some free time. Join her newsletter for bodypositive memes and plenty of dog pics!

Join Phoebe's newsletter at
http://bit.ly/PhoebeAlexanderNews
Facebook group:
https://www.facebook.com/groups/PhoebesAngels

facebook.com/phoebealexanderauthor
instagram.com/authorphoebealexander
tiktok.com/@authorphoebealexander
bookbub.com/authors/phoebe-alexander

Spice Up Our Marriage Series

Project Paradise

Rule Breaker

The Playground

Keeping Secrets

The Ruse

Polyam Fam Series

The Scottish Play

Break a Leg

Alpha Bet Guys Series

A Hole

The Big O

Need the D

Hard F

Ride the C

Standalones

Authority Issues

Clean Grammar for Dirty Minds

www.ingramcontent.com/pod-product-compliance
Lightning Source LLC
Chambersburg PA
CBHW061812190726
48289CB00007B/2172